Pri

Price: Polestarr

Jonathan C. Crouch

"A high-octane adventure where the stakes are higher than anyone possibly imagined"

Price: Polestarr

Coming Soon:
More Adventures with Dr Adam Price.

Join the World of Dr Adam Price at:
PriceWorldNovel.co.uk

Jonathan C. Crouch

Dedications

For Max & Georgie

For Katie, Ro & Charlie

With love & thanks

To Dad - my biggest fan

Foreword

Price: Polestarr - More page turning adventures with Dr Adam Price & his friends.

After the thrilling success of my debut novel - Price: World, which saw our hero battle with an evil Arab oil baron, intent on stealing the Dr's new fusion reactor invention for himself, readers were quickly asking if there was going to be another novel?

One of the biggest problems I've encountered as a new Author, is how to stop your mind writing scenarios and plot lines for the next book, rather than the one you're actually writing at the time.

So it was with Price: World when my thoughts often turned to its follow-up, which you're now about to read.

Price: Polestarr is an all new adventure story, with a new & bigger villain, even more deadly chases and more exciting and stunning locations than its predecessor.

Once again, Dr Adam Price faces peril & danger at every turn in this fast paced action adventure story, joined by his best friend 'Mate', journalist Heather Lightly and newcomer, climatologist, Dr Wednesday

Week, as they try to stop a billionaire industrialist from destroying the World.

Let the adventure begin again!

Jonathan C. Crouch.

Excerpt...

The two missiles passed close to their underbelly and exploded in a nearby cloud formation, but already the fighter pilots had unleashed a further bevy of ballistics at them, and this time, they seemed to have anticipated the i8's avoidance tactics as the two rockets headed for different points in the sky around the i8.

As Adam banked hard to avoid the first rocket, which exploded shockingly close to the car, throwing it off course and peppering the body and windows with shrapnel, so the second missile from the latest volley, correctly positioned itself for impact and the tell-tale warning lights and sound on the i8's main console warned Adam & Wednesday of imminent destruction.

At the last possible moment before impact, Adam dropped the nano-shielding that covered the wheel arches and under-belly of the car.

The sudden shift in aerodynamics threw the car into a wild, gyrating spin, whilst the missile exploded within inches of the rear of the car, causing it to oscillate even more wildly as part of the wing mechanism was worn away. Now the i8 was nothing more than a paper dart, falling to Earth at an alarming rate from which there could be no recovery. All of the instruments told Adam the same inescapable truth. The i8 was going to crash or break up in the sky first.

Price: Polestarr

Contents

Chapter 1

1. The Gathering.

Dr Adam Price was reclined on a huge sofa, watching the News Channel on a large curved screen television. A long dormant Volcano had erupted off the coast of South America, located amongst a cluster of small islands, causing a local Tsunami and throwing hot ash high into the atmosphere, disrupting sea vessels and airplanes alike.

Climate experts had been wheeled out by the news teams, to give their appraisal of the likely ecological damage to the sensitive jungle and coral eco-systems. Each had wearily repeated their earlier dire warnings of, as yet, untold and irreversible scenarios.

The report concluded with the live broadcast cutting back to the studio, where a solemn faced anchor repeated the reports that all of the Islands inhabitants had been evacuated in time by the drilling corporation that owned the small island.

Adam reached for the small remote and switched the television off. Rising up and throwing the device behind him towards the sofa, he walked over to the large curving wall of glass that took up almost the entire wall. Gazing thoughtfully out over the sweeping fields of corn; wind turbines spinning in the evening breeze, he finally made some internal decision and turned and walked out to the hallway with purpose.

This was his new home. Perched on the soft, chalk hills above Cambridge with views that stretched on a clear day to London, over 40 miles away, and in the other direction Ely Cathedral.

He'd finally been persuaded to leave the underground home he'd built, and live, as Heather had put it, back amongst people. Where once a derelict cottage had sat was now a smooth single-storey structure of curving white walls and glass. The roof was a living eco-system covered with Adam's latest invention, a solar panel with a 90% conversion efficiency.

The inner entrance hallway featured a large perpetual waterfall of Adam's own design, the water flowing from a rolled, copper edge, forming a curtain of heavy water which was silently directed by suction into the frothing, bubbling surface of a deep looking pool.

Large pieces of stone lined either side of the waterfall, which was at least 20ft high, and added to the whole aesthetic with plants growing amongst the cracks. Amongst the more austere surroundings of the home, it was a pure slice of almost tropical paradise.

A small polished rail of stainless steel encircled the whole centre-piece which Adam reached for as he approached the fountain. Touching the rail, immediately the curtain of water began to part in the middle as a small footplate appeared in the centre of the pool. At the same time the hand-rail parted in the middle as it telescopically withdrew to either side.

Beyond the parting in the water curtain, which continued to fall noisily and unimpeded, another door, like that of a small lift, slid open.

The whole transformation took mere seconds, and Adam hardly had to break his initial stride as he walked calmly across the dry entrance to the waiting door, already open to receive him.

Before he'd even entered the small lift, the fountain was already returning to normal, the rail re-appeared, as sturdy as ever, and the water resumed its relentless cycle, completely hiding the stainless lift door.

The lift travelled downwards and with a slight bump that made the passenger feel almost weightless for a split second, stopped. Adam stepped out into the cool air of the chalk tunnel the lift had deposited him in.

Walking quickly, Adam traversed the short stretch of connecting corridor and entered the more familiar surroundings of his old home - the secret base under the old barn and wind turbines he'd gazed on earlier.

The living quarters were now no longer necessary and had been converted into a large training arena.

Adam checked his watch. Mate had been due back over an hour ago and it was unlike him to be late. Worrying that Mate had run into difficulties, Adam turned to AMIe - the computer system that aided him on his adventures and requested a location fix on his oldest and closest friend.

***

At 24, Ruby felt a seasoned veteran of climate marches and rallies, and had placards and banners ready to go by the front door of her small, rented first-floor flat in one of London's outer neighbourhoods.

No designer interiors or fashionable boutiques here. Just the daily grime of a fume choked city from a bygone age, with soot accumulations and weather stains that refused to budge, despite the very occasional cleaning initiatives of the local borough.

She checked the small shoulder bag she was taking with her, laced up her boots and deciding against taking a jacket (more stuff to burden and weigh her down), collected the handful of neatly painted placards and headed down the stairs. Touching the small jewelled pin on her lapel - the sparkling ruby that had given her, her name and the only tangible link to a Mother she'd never known, she let the front door swing shut by itself.

Once out on the street, she studied the prevailing cloud cover with a more hopeful than authoritative self-prediction that the grey clouds would soon pass, before setting off.

Walking quickly, stopping occasionally to re-shuffle the placards into a more manageable stack, she made her way to the nearest bus shelter and glancing at the small Timex watch on her wrist, waited patiently for the '64 to arrive.

A large crowd of some two thousand people had already congregated at Hyde Park by the time the bus dropped her off. The Police were out in force - to be expected given the publicity the march had received in the national news coverage.

She quickly spotted a small knot of protestors she knew and forced her way through the crowd towards them. They all embraced and then stood back to admire the placards she'd worked on so diligently the night before.

"World Against Warming" with the first letter of each word symmetrically threaded together, the 'A' standing out in contrasting red paint against the jet black 'W'

Other slogans like "Cool It", the words circling a globe with a sweaty face and a caricature of the Prime Minister with the words "Their Lies Poison the Earth".

She'd just unfurled the long 'WAW' banner she'd planned to carry with one of the others, when a voice carried by a megaphone announced they were off.

With much cheering and applause, the army of protestors set off for Parliament, news photographers running backwards to snap photos of the march and Police, some in riot gear, others on horse-back, followed at a respectful distance with others on foot patrol, their fluorescent jackets forming painted lines either side and keeping up with the crowd.

Further along the route the protest was taking, a large transit van had pulled up in a back street normally reserved for unloading. Inside the back of the van, a small group checked their own bags as they prepared to jump down from the back doors and mingle with the approaching climate protestors.

Unlike Ruby though, their bags contained petrol bombs, smoke grenades and up their sleeves, each had a baseball club secreted.

The Children of WAW had decided that the time for peaceful protest was over. Dissenting voices had urged a more confrontational approach, something to make the politicians sit up & listen and take global warming more seriously, beyond the empty promises of cutting this and reducing that.

Pie-crust promises one of the protestors had said raising a smile from those who remembered Mary Poppins, but that was long ago.

Now an unknown source of wealth and means was funding their protests and the van and weapons had been waiting for them, right where the man had said.

All the politicians, business leaders and even scientists had failed them. Only one former Government energy advisor had appeared to care with his proposals of developing a new energy source, but even that had fell on deaf ears until the work claimed his life.

One of the men slid a small hatch on the driver's cab back and peered down towards the end of the street, where the peaceful protesters would pass in a matter of minutes, Time to go!

Jumping down from the back of the van, the small army moved quickly, keeping to the shadows of the building fronts and the occasional over-hanging awning.

Their timing was perfect. As they reached the end of the street, so the protestors and the accompanying Police cordon intersected with them.

Nodding to each other, they drew petrol bombs and turning away to light them, threw them quickly at the line of Police leading the way.

Orange flames suddenly sprung up everywhere as the home-made bombs burst and sent flaming spirits over the un-prepared Police. Protestors shrieked in fear and all hell broke loose, as colleagues rushed to extinguish those whose clothing was on fire, smothering flames with their own jackets.

The stench of burning fuel was everywhere.

Now smoke bombs landed amongst the crowd, which had already started turning every which-way in panic, as each searched for any path of escape.

Amidst so much screaming and shrieking, the crowd stampeded.

As some tripped and fell to the ground, others ran over them, knocking them to the ground again, in the melee.

Whilst the Children of WAW escaped back the way they'd came, the Police, too busy dealing with the aftermath of the panic and helping those wounded or crushed, missed them completely.

The crowd continued its headlong scramble, only slowing when the crowd emerged from the confines of the tight London streets, and once again entered the park.

At the scene where the violence had erupted, Police Officers and forensic specialists were already scouring the ground for clues, stopping to check for non-existent pulses on the fallen bodies they encountered.

One Officer picked through the scattered debris of belongings. Finding the end of a long, painted banner, scorched and torn, he tugged it as he wound it in, the fabric leading him to the body of a young woman, one hand still clutching the banner to her tightly, the other clutching a small ruby pin.

Jonathan C. Crouch

Chapter 2

2. Space Jigsaw.

Mate had taken one of the electric motorbikes and wound his way across country to a large industrial complex on the outskirts of Milton Keynes, owned by Tek Corp. A large multi-national company with interests in oil & mineral mining, satellites and ecological science with particular initiatives aimed at studying global warming.

The head of the private company, Winston Tek was publicly critical of the World's government failures to deal with the dangers of rising temperatures and had devoted a substantial amount of his own private income to studying and acting on climate change.

When interviewed, he always declared it "his duty to act". He was lauded by climate protestors as a hero and feared by industry leaders and politicians alike. He was ruthless, dedicated and driven and had the wealth to make him independent of both.

Mate had left the bike in a small copse on the opposite side of a hill to the outer perimeter fence.

Checking he hadn't been spotted, he unclipped the full face mask he was wearing, and began to dissolve, leaving the suit in a small crumpled heap next to the bike.

Now he was free of the suit, he had to work quickly, before he dissipated completely. Floating several feet above the ground, he passed through the outer fence and crossed the access road towards a nearby doorway.

Security cameras monitored the entrance but they were completely in-effective on him. As he simply drifted through the closed door into the dimly lit corridor beyond, bare, save for a few grey doors on either side.

Floating down to the furthest door, he looked inside the room and saw a large desk, with computer screen and phone. A small glass trophy stood to one side, with an acorn engraved into the glass, giving a 3d effect.

The computer screen was on and Mate went through the desk to see what was on the screen.

Concentrating hard, he managed to solidify his right hand enough to move the computer mouse.

Clicking and opening files, he quickly located the material Adam had asked him to get. Several blueprints and schematics of a satellite, with hand written annotations and arrows pointing to various points for emphasis.

Hearing noises in the corridor, Mate quickly closed the open files and dissolved his hand, just in time as two burly security guards peered into the office. Satisfied it was empty, they closed the door behind them and continued to check the other doors & rooms before turning the corner at the far end, their boot steps receding into the distance.

Mate listened for a minute at the door, before passing through the door and back into the corridor. He was just at the outside entrance when an alarm sounded. Obviously, unauthorised activity on the computers was secretly monitored. Now foot-steps could be heard coming back towards him, running.

Taking a deep breath, Mate turned and passed through the metal door and was across the road and over the metal fence before the guards reached the end office.

Once back at the bike, he tried to reform back into the suit, but to no avail. The solidifying of his hand had used up more of his energy than he thought. Slowly the surrounding fields became a blur like a watercolour running off the paper in a storm, as Mate felt the last few fleeting moments slip away and he dissolved completely.

***

The Vandenberg Space Force Base lies northwest of Los Angeles in the United States. With the Los Padres National Park forest far behind and the Ocean of the North Pacific to the front, its isolation made it a popular choice for private companies looking to launch their own satellites into low Earth orbits.

The Tek Corp had its own buildings and division there, with personnel in construction, electronics, guidance and launch room specialities.

During the last 14 months, they'd successfully launched a series of climate satellites. Today, the 15th and final satellite would be launched, to link up with the other 14 in a necklace of satellites orbiting around the Earth, providing the first, real time climate & weather data available to the scientific communities and climate modellers.

The whole project, named Polestarr, was the brainchild of Winston Tek and was being entirely funded by him.

Winston Tek himself was there, in the control room as the final minutes of the countdown began.

The previous built in 'hold' periods had all passed smoothly and the booster rocket that would lift the satellite to the correct orbit was showing all systems go.

With a final go / no-go for launch, the flight director called off the various launch specialists and when the launchpad controller gave the final 'go', the countdown was into the last 60 seconds.

At exactly the right moment, boosters ignited and steel gantries fell back as the rocket and its precious cargo were carried up into the brilliant blue sky on a blazing trail of flames.

Despite the almost routine-ness of the launch, the ground controllers cheered & applauded, and the flight director turned towards Winston, flashing him a big grin and the thumbs up sign.

The booster shut off on schedule and small thrusters pushed the satellite away from the main rocket body, that would fall back to land in the ocean. Once clear, a series of solar panel arrays sprung outward, like umbrellas being put up, in a precision ballet of mechanical co-ordination.

At the Tek offices within the Vandenberg complex, controllers monitoring the satellite, manoeuvred it into place, amongst the other 14 evenly spaced satellites, and began a series of commissioning procedures to bring the last piece of this gigantic space jigsaw puzzle online.

Escaping the roomful of delegates and directors, Winston Tek made his way to a smaller entrance, just off of the main entrance lobby to a waiting car - a large white electrically powered SUV.

A driver patiently stood, holding the rear door open for him, and once he'd taken his seat, the driver had closed the door and climbed behind the wheel.

"Where to Mr Tek"?

"Los Angeles airport - and hurry!".

Taking his smart phone from inside his jacket pocket, he typed a quick message 'Phase one complete' before putting the device away and settling back into the leather seats of the air-conditioned car, for the journey back into the city.

***

Adam Price had watched the launch of the last Polestarr satellite after hacking into the Mission Control cameras and launch data screens for himself, from the cave HQ.

His own tracking was already following the other Polestarr satellites, monitoring not only their position, but the data streams they were producing.

AMIe was already running the data through climate simulations and had projected a 3d image of the Earth, rotating lazily as the data showed current weather patterns and an overlay projection showed future predictions of weather and temperature.

He was gazing at the projection when AMIe interrupted him with "Heather is at the front door". Heather Lightly, the reporter that had followed his and Mate's movements previously, as they'd foiled the plans of Arab oil baron Mehat, to steal Adam's fusion reactor invention and use it to take control of the World's energy supplies.

Heather had joined him and Mate on their adventures and fully aware of the secrets Adam and Mate kept, had sworn to keep them to herself, in return for the occasional exclusive story of course.

Adam left the 3d model and took the lift back to the house level. Moving out, he reached the front door before Heather pressed the doorbell again.

Swinging the door open wide, he smiled and welcomed her inside. She returned the smile and placing her jacket & bag on a chair, immediately asked how he was? "I'm enjoying the quiet life above ground". "And Mate?" "he's out at the moment. I was expecting him back at any time now".

They moved into the lounge area and Adam motioned Heather to sit on the opposite sofa. "Now how can I help you?", and so Heather had begun by telling him of her investigations into the possible funding of recent climate marches, and a climatologist that had contacted her with what she claimed was worrying evidence that the Polestarr data was inaccurate.

"My journalistic instinct tells me the two might be related, but by who or what for I've no idea".

"What's this climatologist's name?" Adam asked.

"Wednesday Week" replied Heather, giggling. "Apparently, her Dad was a huge Undertones fan and with a surname like Week..".

"She worked for the Tek Corp didn't she?"

"Yes. She's their former chief climate scientist".

"I was watching their latest satellite launch earlier. That's fifteen he's launched now, supposedly to provide real time weather & climate data on the whole World".

"You're not convinced?" Replied Heather, frowning.

"No, I'm not, Something tells me there's more to it than just climate mapping. I sent Mate in to investigate but as I said, he's not back yet. In fact, he's overdue and I was starting to get worried."

***

The small wooded area around the motorbike was still, with hardly a breath of air, when the smaller branches began swaying uncharacteristically and the leaves rustled as though caught in a small tornado.

Gradually, the suit laying in the grass and Cow parsley began to expand and fill out as finally the gloved hand pulled the face mask in place and the figure mounted the electric bike and rode silently away.

A little over an hour later and Mate was pulling into the driveway of Jupiter House. Pulling the motorbike up on its centre stand at the side of the front door, he walked into the house to find Heather and Adam in the lounge, watching the earlier launch on the national news.

At sight of him, Heather jumped up with a squeal and ran to embrace him. Throwing her arms around him, she said how she'd missed him, working away in London and on various assignments.

"We were starting to get worried. Where have you been?" She finally exclaimed.

"I ran out of time and lost cohesion just as I'd got out of the compound".

"I thought we'd got the timings right on that front" injected Adam.

"We had, it's just I had to re-materialise my hand to operate a computer and that really seemed to zap me. I barely made it out of the grounds."

"Who's compound?" Asked Heather. Adam looked at Mate and shook his head. Heather spotted the almost in-perceptible movement and added "or shouldn't I ask?".

"Just a little project I'm working on" replied Adam, easily.

Heather shrugged off the inference that she shouldn't ask any more questions and the three sat and chatted until late into the evening.

Chapter 3

3. Wednesday Week.

The evening had only broken up when Mate had started to loose cohesion and as Adam walked Heather outside to her car, she asked Adam if he'd agree to meet with Dr Wednesday Week.

Adam had said he'd be intrigued to find out more and a time for the following day was agreed on. Adam watched her drive off, the red tail-lights of the electric Mini Cooper receding quickly up the dark village street.

The following morning and Adam was pouring over copies of the blueprints Mate had seen in the Tek Corp offices. Making his own notes and drawing lines to various points on the schematics, when AMIe informed him that Dr Week had arrived.

Quickly putting the plans away, he fairly ran to the front door and opened it to the delightful Ms Week.

She stood a little awkwardly as if unsure whether to enter or turn & run, but Adam's welcome was so warm and enthusiastic, she didn't give the notion of running a second thought, and passed through the entranceway.

After polite enquires as to each others health, Wednesday began by saying "I know you by reputation of course, and the research you've conducted yourself, into alternative fuels and renewable energy. I didn't know quite what to do with the discovery I've made or who to show it to, that I wouldn't be laughed at".

"I promise I won't laugh" replied Adam. He was totally captivated by her and would have quite easily told her everything about his secret HQ and the inventions he had without a second thought.

Instead, he settled for asking her what she'd found.

"I was reviewing the historical data from the first Polestarr satellites that were launched and I came across an anomaly. The data that was being recorded back on Earth was way off what was actually happening on the surface.

I've invested my own money into a small sea temperature experiment, with several measuring buoys located around the path of the North Atlantic Drift, and they tell me that temperatures have remained steady, whereas the Polestarr data says we've experienced a slight drop. I can't account for it."

Price: Polestarr

"Isn't the temperature dropping a good thing?" Asked Adam.

"Normally yes but if the data tells you its dropping, then the conclusion is that your reduction methods are working and restrictions on any carbon activity get loosened.

And if that's based on false data, then any lifting of restrictions could have serious consequences".

She'd barely stopped talking when her mobile phone bleeped. Frowning, she picked it up and swiped the screen. Showing it to Adam, she pointed out what was happening. The screen showed a small map of the top of the Atlantic Ocean, the landmass in faint outline, and a broad moving ribbon showing the Drift. Of four pinpoints, one was flashing. She touched the point and a flow of data appeared underneath. Temperature, salinity, direction, current strength etc.

"This is what I meant" she exclaimed. "The temperature in this section of the Drift just rose, in keeping with the predictions for this time of year as more of the coast of Greenland thaws with the strength of the Sun. Compare that with the data from Polestarr and it recorded no rise."

Jonathan C. Crouch

"What do you need?" Asked Adam. "Would being closer to the actual point of collection be helpful?".

"If we could get close enough to the point the date is generated, then perhaps we could figure what the problem is, and correct it".

"And", finished Adam, "discover if there's anything more sinister at work here".

Adam had already made up his mind, that Wednesday Week could be trusted and deciding that not a moment more could be wasted, asked her if she fancied taking a little drive?

"My car's just outside" she began.

"You don't mind if we take mine?" Replied Adam, taking her hand and heading for the large sporty BMW car parked to the side of the house.

Wednesday hardly had time to marvel at the high-tech interior of the car, which Adam had pulled her towards before the gull-wing doors started to close.

Large screens and displays came to life and Adam had hardly closed his own door before he drove out onto village lane, and headed for its long deserted section.

Price: Polestarr

Amidst the revelations, Wednesday managed to ask "where are you taking me?"

"Well" said Adam, turning to look at her, "I thought we'd better do something about accessing that data source you spoke of, however, I think we need to get to the exact point its generated from".

"You mean, the satellite itself?" Asked Wednesday incredulously.

"I do" replied Adam, laughing.

As the i8 cleared the last bend out of the village, so AMIe reported that radar was all clear.

"Standby to change to flight mode" said Adam, and pressing a series of buttons, made the delta-shaped wings fold out from underneath the car as a small rocket engine appeared from the rear of the car and with a sudden burst of speed, the car shot up into the afternoon sky.

Wednesday had only just begun to relax from her arms out-stretched pose, braced against the door and centre console handles, when the car had first took off, however it became clear they weren't levelling off, but continuing the steep curving climb towards space itself.

Jonathan C. Crouch

The aerodynamic shape of the car, aided by the nano-shell technology that Adam had created, to cover over the wheel arches and the underneath of the car, meant it was able to slip smoothly through the atmosphere without the usual punishing G-Forces an Astronaut might experience, and enter the thinning atmosphere of space itself.

Now the Earth took on the curvature of its surface from so high up and weather patterns emerged in the cloud cover as they headed deeper out into the dark void ahead.

As Adam cut back the power, so Wednesday experienced the euphoria of weightlessness, the only thing keeping her in her seat, the passive restraint system.

Her phone floated lazily past her face as she tore her gaze away from the majestic panorama of the Earth to look at Adam.

He was looking at her, beaming. One hand on the steering wheel, the other touching various buttons on the touch screens whilst AMIe kept up a running commentary on the cars status and heading.

"You weren't kidding when you said you wanted a closer look" she finally managed to say, "and this wonderful car of yours; you can actually fly into space!".

And so Adam told her everything, the explosion in Scotland, how Mate had found him, their near death fight with Mehat, and the very end when Mate had got caught and died in the fusion liquid, only to re-appear later at the house.

A small blip appeared on the centre most screen and grew in size as Adam pointed to a point of light outside in front of them, hanging in the void of space. As the car approached it, Wednesday could see it was a satellite, like a child might draw one. A long cylindrical body with solar panels fanning outwards and a small antenna at one end facing the Earth.

Adam manoeuvred the i8 so it was directly between the antenna and the Earth, and with AMIe's help, patched the car into the data stream the satellite was recording from the point on the Earth's surface it was directed at.

Data started scrolling across the screen. "Now" said Adam. "Lets compare that with the data being transmitted back to Earth", flipping another button as he spoke and bringing a second monitor display to life.

Wednesday looked at the data and back at Adam and was about to speak when Adam spoke exactly what she was thinking. The data the satellite was recording matched her own buoy readings, whilst the data being sent to Earth was self-adjusting to record no alterations.

The data was being manipulated but why and exactly by who, were a complete mystery.

Chapter 4

4. Evasive Manoeuvre.

At Tek Corp's Vandenberg headquarters, one of the station monitors motioned his supervisor over to look at his screen. Pointing to various points, the supervisor nodded and returning to his own desk, picked up the phone and spoke quickly to the person on the other end of the call.

Calling up the data on his own screen, the supervisor rattled off a serious of co-ordinates before hanging up.

Winston Tek didn't replace the phone's handset, but instead, pressed the end call button and dialled another number quickly. "We may have a situation. Someone or something has briefly intercepted the data stream from Polestarr satellite number 10. I need whatever it is intercepted and shot down. I presume it is some kind of drone collecting classified data from the Polestarr network. It cannot be allowed to land back or transmit data of any kind.".

The voice on the other end of the line was talking to which Winston only nodded in reply, presumably offering a solution to the problem of the Drone.

"Thank you General for the Air Force assistance".

At the USAF air base at Alconbury, near Peterborough UK, a pair of Stealth Jets were being hurriedly prepped for take-off.

The two pilots were being briefed as the jets were being readied. A drone or other device was plotted as entering UK airspace from low orbit, having interfered with a private satellite.

Their orders were to intercept at high altitude and shoot it down.

As the jets took off, so operations in the underground flight control centre were monitoring the jets positions and providing solutions to the earliest possible intercept point. From his own private offices, Winston Tek watched the same information as the airborne chase unfolded, with an ever so slight look of excitement on the otherwise impassive features.

Adam was already firing the i8's retro thrusters for the return journey home when AMIe announced the two jets on radar, closing on their position fast.

Wednesday looked at Adam with alarm and said "they won't open fire on us surely?".

"I honestly don't know" replied Adam grimly. I suspect Tek Corp detected us somehow and Winston Tek has the resources to cajole a friendly force into shooting down anything considered a threat". "AMIe plot evasive manoeuvres and engage on my mark. Lets hope we can dodge or outrun anything they send after us".

Now the i8 was caught in the fiery envelope of re-entry, as the dark, starry sky gave way to the more familiar clear blue of the Earth's outer atmosphere. Down they continued as AMIe updated the radar information on the as yet unknown aircraft chasing them.

"I delayed our re-entry which has bought us in a little off the original point. It should have thrown them momentarily". Adam winked at Wednesday and took the controls. "Stand by decoys" as two extra blips suddenly appeared on the radar screen, heading straight for them. Rockets! "Hard over AMIe and engage evasive flight pattern". The i8 pitched and went into a steep twisting dive as Wednesday hung on, quite unprepared for the sudden change of direction. One that was beyond any normal aircraft.

The two pilots watched as their instruments told them the missiles had missed the target and exploded harmlessly out of range. Already as their weapons computers were plotting new firing points, so Adam had put the i8 into a steep parabolic climb. Again, two missiles were heading straight for them, whilst the jets continued to close the distance between them and the i8. Again, Adam threw the car into a steep dive, twisting left & right as they went, the speed eating up altitude at an alarming rate. Already the ground was taking on the characteristic look of fields and forests.

The two missiles passed close to their underbelly and exploded in a nearby cloud formation, but already the fighter pilots had unleashed a further bevy of ballistics at them, and this time, they seemed to have anticipated the i8's avoidance tactics as the two rockets headed for different points in the sky around the i8.

As Adam banked hard to avoid the first rocket, which exploded shockingly close to the car, throwing it off course and peppering the body and windows with shrapnel, so the second missile from the latest volley, correctly positioned itself for impact and the tell-tale warning lights and sound on the i8's main console warned Adam & Wednesday of imminent destruction.

Price: Polestarr

At the last possible moment before impact, Adam dropped the nano-shielding that covered the wheel arches and under-belly of the car.

The sudden shift in aerodynamics threw the car into a wild, gyrating spin, whilst the missile exploded within inches of the rear of the car, causing it to oscillate even more wildly as part of the wing mechanism was worn away. Now the i8 was nothing more than a paper dart, falling to Earth at an alarming rate from which there could be no recovery. All of the instruments told Adam the same inescapable truth. The i8 was going to crash or break up in the sky first.

There was only one thing for it. They were going to have to eject. "Eject?" Screamed Wednesday. "I've never used a parachute before".

"Don't worry" replied Adam, "My parachutes are self-guiding & self-flying. They'll set us down as light as a feather. That is if we can get out before the car breaks up around us" and the warning was not in vain for already, pieces of the cars outer skin were being peeled away, like an onion, layer by layer.

"AMIe, prepare for ejection" spoke Adam quickly, adding "lets just hope the electronics haven't been damaged". "Confirmed" said AMIe in reply. "Chairs activating in 5,4,3,2,1... now".

Jonathan C. Crouch

As the gull-wing doors blew away, the two front seats slid out on steel booms, so that Wednesday found herself literally hanging in thin air. Glancing across she could see Adam's seat had done the same.

"Now" said AMIe cooly and suddenly, Wednesday felt her world turn upside down and with a sickening lurch, the seat launched her out into the sky.

Free of the car, the passenger seat she'd been sitting in righted itself and began falling, before a large grey parachute suddenly deployed above her and began the slow drift towards the ground.

Now that her heart had stopped pounding, she looked around her and could see Adam's own parachute around 300 yards away from her, but reassuringly moving ever closer to her.

Below, the i8 had already hit the ground with a small cloud of dust kicked up into the air. If she'd been expecting an large explosion, she was disappointed, until she remembered the car had been electric and had no fuel tanks to ignite and explode.

Suddenly, Adam was at her side, his own parachute mirroring hers in perfect unison as the pair weaved and rode the air currents, heading towards a small meadow that bordered a deserted road.

Price: Polestarr

Adam had been right, as the last few meters of ground rose to meet them, the parachutes controlling flaps and slits in the canopy, lowered them both to a standing position. As their feet hit the ground, the parachute and car seats fell away from them, the top of the car seat automatically winding in the parachute, to stop it being blown away.

Adam walked over to her "are you alight?" He enquired taking her hand as he did.

Yes" she replied, a little shaky but quickly regaining some composure, she replied "it's a good job you had those seats".

"Yes but I'd never expected to have to use them". "C'mon, we need to get to the car".

A brisk walk of 10 minutes bought them both to the spot where the i8 had ended up. A small, hollow, with gnarly trees forming an amphitheatre of bare, damp soil, the sun hardly breaking through the tree canopy that surrounded the spot.

In the centre was what was left of the i8 and it wasn't much at that. Save for a strange metallic case that seemed undamaged, the rest of the car was a broken shell, with pieces of metal and polycarbonate littering the strange little natural hollow. The monitors were all dead or smashed or both.

Only a small red LED blinked repeatedly and Adam reached for it through the twisted corpse of the car.

Pressing the small light, AMIe's voice announced that the S.O.S had been sent with co-ordinates for their location. Help was already on its way, and should be there within 10 minutes.

8 Minutes later and a small convoy of trucks and SUV's appeared on the road, travelling towards them, as the first wagon pulled up, Soldiers leapt down from the opened tail gate and took up defensive positions around the outer perimeter, their guns trained away from the small wooded area.

Another group of soldiers appeared, walking towards them. In their midst was an elderly gentleman, seemingly out of place in his suit & bowler hat. A walking cane completed the austere ensemble, but as he got closer to Adam so his face broke out into a smile and he and Adam shook hands.

Adam turned and introduced him to Wednesday. The old gent bowed slightly, touching the rim of his hat, before turning back towards Adam.

"You've got yourself and Ms Week into quite a mess it seems. I presume it was you the Polestarr tracking identified as an intruder". It was a statement not a question, and one said with just the hint of annoyance.

"When are going to learn you can't simply interfere with things in this manner? There are protocols to observe, channels to go through and sometimes when the answer is NO, you have to accept that".

Already the remaining Soldiers were recovering bits of the i8 and throwing them into the back of one of the trucks. With the help of a small, hydraulic crane, the larger pieces were being lifted and placed in the back of a covered wagon.

"Of course, the pieces will be returned to you eventually" smiled the Old Man.

"I didn't think you'd waste the opportunity" returned Adam, "and I doubt your average breakdown cover comes so well equipped".

"Now why don't you and Ms Week here, escort and old man back to his car and we can talk on the way back".

Adam turned to look behind them. There wasn't so much as a blade of grass out of place that would suggest the i8 had ever crashed there.

As they drove back to London, so Adam told the Old Man about Wednesday coming to visit him, her concerns about the Polestarr data and her own personal Drift studies.

Deciding that a close inspection of one of the Satellites itself much yield answers, they hadn't wasted a moment in taking off.

It was only as they'd prepared to re-enter Earth's atmosphere that the two jets had launched their attack. One they'd been luck to escape from with their lives.

"And did your covert analysis reveal anything useful?" Queried the old gentleman with a look that suggested the question was rhetorical. Wednesday spoke first "Yes it did. It seems the data being transmitted to Earth is adjusted at the point of collection, namely the satellite itself. If all fifteen satellites are doing the same thing, then the collective data is wildly out".

"But why tamper with readings and make them suggest the Earth is cooling rather than warming up?". It was Adam who answered grimly "because if the previously projected readings were wrong and had mistakenly implied the Earth was warming faster than it actually is, then Governments will act accordingly and slow or even reverse some of their climate decisions, including those policies that control oil, gas and mineral drilling and mining".

"But to what purpose?" Countered Wednesday. Who would want to go to such extremes just to relax the climate policy of the World's leaders. Some un-developed country being strangled by the restrictions on burning fossil fuels, or a more developed country that will be bankrupted by the investment in green technology implementation?".

"I think", replied Adam, "that the answer is more likely to be an individual or organisation, intent on building a monopoly that relies on more traditional means of energy, either its usage or exploration. A good place to start looking would be your old boss, Winston Tek. He is the one after all, that developed and launched the Polestarr system".

Jonathan C. Crouch

Chapter 5

5. Tek's Game.

Winston Tek hung up the phone, pondering the report he'd just received from his men in England, who'd traced the unidentified craft that had intercepted one of his satellites and after a brief dog-fight with the British RAF, had been shot down, and crashed in the county of Sussex.

Although they were sure they'd located the very spot, there was no trace of any wreckage or that there had ever been any crash-landing at all.

The surrounding trees and bushes showed no signs of any damage or heat and the ground itself was perfectly preserved.

Only a spectral reading had indicated a trace of an unknown gaseous element, and that was being investigated further.

He would report again in 24 hours with an update.

He whirled round in his seat, to face the wall behind his desk, which held a large ornate framed painting, depicting one of the classic naval battles of the Napoleonic Wars, with a French and British war ship firing cannons at close quarters, the smoke tinged with the orange flare of the gunpowder discharge, in the broadside onslaught.

It was both evocative and fascinating.

Pressing a biometric button set in in the padded arm of the chair, the wall and painting slid silently to one side, to reveal a bank of screens. The central one flickered briefly and came to life showing the face of a man in his mid-thirties. Unshaven and short haired. He was dressed in a black combat suit. Behind him, personnel were either working at desks, work benches or loading vehicles with a variety of different size crates. The whole scene was orderly, almost military like.

"You did well" started Tek. "The British newspapers are full of stories of the Children of WAW, and the tragic loss of life in the most recent climate protest in London.

It's time to step-up the campaign. Do you have your next target arranged?".

"We do". "Another rally is set to go-ahead in Paris this coming weekend. The crowds are expected to be even larger than the London gathering. My team are already in one of Paris' less affluential suburbs, and will be in position on time. As per your instructions, we're stepping up the violence level with some explosives and this time, there will be two teams, one to intercept the head of the march and another covering the main retreat corridor".

"Good, good" nodded Tek, "and afterwards?"

"Rome the following week. For that we have something really spectacular planned, but I don't want to spoil the surprise".

"WAW out" and the multi-screens disappeared as the wall reverted to the old oil painting.

Adam and Wednesday had been driven back to his home by one of the old gentleman's chauffeurs. As he reversed out of the driveway, so Adam only waited to see him drive off before turning and following Wednesday into the house.

They walked through to the lounge and joined Mate who was suitably suited for the sake of the visitor, AMIe had warned him was approaching the house with Adam.

He rose to meet them and extended his hand to shake Wednesday's, who on seeing the stranger had turned alarmed to Adam.

"Meet my very good friend and colleague, Mark or Mate, as he's more usually called. Mate unfortunately suffered an accident which left him with some severe scars, so now he wears this specially adapted suit.".

"I'm very pleased to meet you" said Mate, repeating the movement of extending his arm to shake her hand. This time, she took it in a polite handshake, before sitting beside Mate on one of the sofa's.

"I was beginning to get worried when you weren't back, and you left so quickly too" The last Mate said with a slight nod at Wednesday.

"We decided it couldn't wait" replied Adam as he and Wednesday launched into an account of their adventure, including being shot down, and the subsequent meeting with the old gentleman back in London.

When they'd finished recounting the story up to the silent drive back to the house, Mate spoke "And he's no idea who authorised the RAF intercept? What are you going to do now the i8 is out of action?".

"Well, I'll have to bring the development forward of the i8 v3 I've been working on, but more importantly, I think we have to investigate Winston Tek a little more closely and try and stall the Ministry's

Price: Polestarr

efforts trying to pick apart the secrets of the i8 they've now got in their possession.

The second I think is a job for you Mate, whilst AMIe and I try to locate where they took the i8 wreckage."

"Wednesday, I need to ask a favour".

"Sure, anything" replied Wednesday, who'd got over the initial shock of Mate's suited appearance, the high collar covering much of the full head mask he was wearing, and looked sewn into the boiler-suit like, one piece garment he was wearing, much like the Astronauts wore on the Space Station.

"I need all the data you can get me on the Polestarr satellites and allowing for the same rate of tampering we witnessed on all 15 satellites, try and gain a World perspective on what's really happening".

"And" he added, rising, "be careful. There's more going on here than just simple data manipulation and until we can figure out to what end this is all for, I don't think any of us are particularly safe".

He crossed over to a set of drawers and removed a small, watch like device. "Here I want you to wear this. Any problems, just press the face twice or whisper 'Help', and either myself or Mate will come running".

"Like the cavalry?" She replied nervously, and reaching for the watch that was an exact replica of her own, immediately removed her old watch and replaced it with the one Adam had given her.

"Don't worry" replied Mate. "When Adam says we'll be there, you can't imagine how quickly that will be".

A little re-assured by Mate's casualness, she turned back to Adam and said "do you really think we're in any danger?".

Adam considered for a moment before he replied, judging that it was best to be absolutely truthful with her. "I think that someone who has gone to the trouble and expense of launching fifteen satellites and had us shot down in flight, should be considered a very dangerous individual, capable of anything".

"Be mindful of your surroundings, you must" croaked Mate, impersonating the voice of the Yoda character from Star Wars. It was a welcome moment of light relief to end the evening on.

They'd both walked Wednesday to her car and as she'd headed away, Adam had turned to Mate and said "C'mon, we've got a lot to do and something tells me, very little time", as both men entered the house and closed the door.

Price: Polestarr

The next day dawned bright an sunny. Adam was sat having breakfast in front of the large panoramic window, watching the clouds causing patterns of shade on the undulating crops of the surrounding fields of corn. Kite's were already wheeling in the warm currents, circling in hunt of prey and high overhead, vapour trails from Airliners at altitude criss-crossed the sky,

Mate had succumbed to the dissipation that evening only after they'd drawn up plans to take on Winston Tek's corporation. Plans that included Adam meeting Tek in person, whilst Mate was going to infiltrate the location of the i8's wreckage and disable any work into the car's capabilities and more importantly, the small fusion reactor contained within the titanium box.

AMIe had a fix on the location, despite the buildings screening and dampening fields, it was a large underground complex on the outskirts of London. To be more precise the old multi-storey car park they had met in before.

Mate would carry a small portable terminal which contained it's own AMIe. The idea being she would integrate with her own self operating system in the wreck as part of their sabotage plans.

Jonathan C. Crouch

Once Mate had gone, Adam had set aside things and taken the hidden lift down to the underground base, where he'd taken up his work on the latest incarnation of the i8. This was a gleaming metallic bronze, and the floor of the car was slightly higher, more like BMW's X6 SUV coupe.

The new I8 was actually a lot further along than Adam had let on and aside from some test-flights, only needed systems calibrations and AMIe's installation to be ready.

With the final download finished, Adam removed the series of cables and plugs from under the i8's engine hood and interior, and stowed them away.

Taking the driver's seat, he pressed the start button, muttering "fingers crossed" as the car came to life.

The car's interior was completely re-styled. Gone were the multiple displays, replaced by a broad sweeping single screen set into the dashboard at the same level as the instruments on a normal car might be found.

Inset into this, was a vertical screen which flowed all the way to the centre console. Over head, another touch-panel lit up with various symbols, depicting flight and other modes the car was capable of.

AMIe's voice filtered through and reported that all systems were green, including the new, more powerful fusion reactor the car was fitted with.

Adam had played with some of the screens and settings before shutting the car down and calling it a night.

Now as he finished breakfast, he dialled Heather's number and after a few rings, her characteristic voice answered sleepily "Heather". "Hi" replied Adam visualising her trying to wake up fully. "I was wondering if you had any plans today?".

"Nothing important" replied a now more awake voice, "why?".

"I was thinking of taking a trip to London, meeting with Winston Tek. I could do with a P.A. if you're interested?"

"You mean Executive Assistant? The answer's yes I'd love to. Where do you want to meet?"

"It's probably best if I travel to you. I'm sending a data file to your email that has all the information on it of what I'll be asking etc. See you in 2 hours".

Two hours later and Adam pulled up outside Heather's flat on one of the Electric bikes. Stowing the helmet and over-jacket, as Heather joined him

59

outside and together they climbed into the waiting taxi.

The short journey across London was uneventful and the normally chatty taxi driver was silent, watching the road ahead carefully.

"So" Heather had begun once the taxi was underway, "What's your sudden interest in Winston Tek?".

"I think" replied Adam, "that he's involved in something that goes beyond just recording the weather. Has Wednesday spoken with you since her visit to me?".

"Only to say that she was grateful for the introduction and your meeting had given her new directions to focus her research on".

Adam quickly filled in Heather own what had happened after she'd left them. At times Heather looked amazed, stunned and worried when Adam described the rocket attack and crash landing. "That's why I'm on the bike, until I can get the car repaired".

"And you think Winston's behind all of this?"

"I do" replied Adam frankly "and its up to me to try and find out what exactly".

Price: Polestarr

The high-rise building in London's Canary Wharf gleamed in the noon sunlight as the taxi pulled up and Adam and Heather got out and headed for the large revolving reception entrance to the office suites.

Once inside the cool atrium, electronic touch devices helped visitors locate the company they'd come to meet.

However there was no need as a small women stood patiently holding a gilt-edged hand written placard which had Adam's and Heather's names on it.

Adam smiled and turned to Heather to gauge her reaction. She took it in her stride and falling into character of a PA, immediately walked up to the woman holding the placard and introduced Adam and herself.

The woman had smiled and introduced herself as Anita, "Mr Tek's personal assistant in London" She made polite conversation asking after their journey as she ushered them towards a central elevator, its doors held open, waiting.

The ride to the 78th floor was in silence and as the lift pinged and the doors swept open, all three stepped out into a lavishly carpeted reception area, soft furnishings had been used to lessen the impact of the modern, all glass & beams construction.

Jonathan C. Crouch

Crossing to a small unmanned desk, Anita pressed an intercom button and spoke softly announcing the visitors arrival.

Immediately, two larger doors flung open and there was Winston Tek striding towards them, a big grin in his face and a large hand out-stretched to greet Adam. "Dr Price and your quite charming assistant, welcome, welcome to my offices." Turning to Anita, he said "please make sure we're not disturbed" and then shepherding them both forward with those huge bear like arms of his, 'Tek, moved the party into his office.

Once seated, he became much more the business man. He was confident yet friendly and moved his large bulk, in its expensive hand-made suit, with considerable grace and light of foot.

As Heather reached into the small satchel she'd carried and took out notebook & pen, so 'Tek began by saying how honoured he was when he received Adam's call, asking for a meeting in person.

"When they told me it was you yourself on the phone, I must admit to being taken by complete surprise. Why sir you are as good as royalty in the scientific community and most of us have heard of your latest accomplishments in fusion reaction."

"Green power" he continued, "is the single most important undertaking that any generation has been charged with undertaking, if mankind is to survive long enough to escape to the stars".

Adam had bowed slightly in recognition of the achievements being named, and replied "I agree, and thats why I wanted to meet you in person, Your Polestarr program is quite exceptional and I was keen to hear first-hand if the data was what you'd expected?".

At this, 'Tek had seemed momentarily off-guard before the slick smile returned and without missing a heart-beat, replied "its everything we dreamt or feared, we would see. The data is generated in real time, making the previous global warming models as obsolete as the dinosaurs. Soon we'll be able to also report weather forecasts and trump even the computerised global weather models as well.

Science will for the first time, be able to make informed, educated actions towards stabilising our planets climate and take positive action to reduce global warming where it is actually occurring.

We have entered a new age of fully predictable weather and warming patterns".

While he spoke and Adam listened intently, Heather had been casting her eye about the office, whilst writing notes, as instructed. The office had all the trappings of a successful business tycoons office - rich furnishings, a comfortable suite off to one side near to the windows and a large oil painting of an old naval battle hung behind the man himself.

As 'Tek finished his oratorial, so Adam spoke "I was privy to a small piece of research that's been tracking currents in the North Atlantic. The temperature data seemed at odds with your own data and I wondered if you might have any insights into the discrepancy?"

"You must tell me the source of this data and I'll have my team investigate it. There could be any number of reasons why their data is inconsistent. The age of their equipment, the manner in which its being collected etc. could all cause a local variation to be reported".

"But surely" replied Adam, "if the data is correct and I saw nothing to contradict it. In fact I even checked it myself to verify it wasn't some miss-recording on antiquated equipment, that's simply been in the sea too long".

"You checked it yourself?" Rumbled 'Tek softly, yet so powerfully as to override Adam's sentence.

A small buzzer sounded on the desk and reaching to cancel it, Tek said apologetically, "I'm sorry but urgent business requires my attention. Look, I'd like to re-assure you (both, he added) of the reliability of the Polestarr program. Why don't you come out to my main data centre and Mission Control in Vandenberg. I think you'll find it answers all your questions. I'll have Anita arrange things with Miss Lightly here." And with an almost dismissive wave of one of his huge hands, waved them towards the doors that Anita had opened, upon the summons.

Before they left the floor, Anita had arranged dates with Heather for them both to visit in America the following week, and waving them goodbye at the lift's entrance, let them both find their own way out to the waiting taxi.

Tek watched them walk across the paved concourse, to the taxi and pull away. So, it had been Dr Price himself who'd interrupted the data flow from one of his satellites, and the Atlantic project he'd referred to was the work of one Dr Wednesday Week, a leading climatologist, who'd once worked for him and was now funded by several green organisations to dis-credit the miss-leading studies of Governments and industry.

Taking a small mobile phone from his pocket, he quickly speed dialled a number and spoke quickly "Dr Wednesday Week has become too much of a liability. It's time we withdrew our professional courtesy".

Chapter 6

6. Wednesday in Peril.

By the time the plain dark coloured van pulled up outside the small industrial complex, it was already growing dark, yet the lights still burnt on the fourth floor, indicating that someone was still working.

The two men got out, and moved carefully towards a small side entrance. Inserting a small lock picking device into the keyhole, the first man had the the door open in less than 10 seconds, whist his colleague had visually scanned the area, keeping watch.

Once inside, they pulled the door closed behind them and moved stealthily through the corridors and partitions towards a central staircase, they knew to be there.

They met no-one and only stopped at the 2nd floor to wait for a cleaner, waving a mechanised floor polisher along, lost in the beat of whatever was piping through the bluetooth ear-pods he was wearing.

Wednesday was sitting, her back to the lab's doorway, comparing data between two large screens and a print out she had on the desk.

Drawing a line through one row of data with a red pen & ruler, she placed both hands in the small of her back and arched backwards.

Climbing off the stool, she walked out into the corridor and climbed the stairs to the 5th floor, which had the better coffee & snack machine than their own floor.

Waiting patiently for her drink to finish pouring she surveyed the brightly coloured and alluring snacks in the adjacent machine, Deciding that she really should abstain from more sugar, she settled for the coffee only and removing it carefully so as not burn her fingers, she turned and tip-toed back the way she'd come.

She was nearly at the bottom of the stairs when she saw the two men searching under counters in the laboratory room, she'd been sat in not 5 minutes previously.

Shrinking back up the stairs, she didn't hesitate in reaching for the special replica watch that Adam had given her and quickly pressed the watch face twice.

Price: Polestarr

Adam had just arrived back at Jupiter House, having said goodnight to Heather earlier, and was all set to fall into one of the comfy sofa's when AMIe interrupted him with "Adam, Dr Week's emergency alarm has been activated".

Mate was already materialised in the suit, as Adam rushed through the hallway and entered the secret lift entrance. Mate joined him and quickly they descended to the dim coolness of the cave corridor.

"Wednesday's alarm has activated. We have to get to her immediately", panted Adam, running for a new large doomed vehicle bay off to the right.

The new i8 was already running, its doors open as the two approached the car. This was the first time Mate had seen the new car and he whistled his approval of the re-designed interior.

Adam was already throwing switches as the car, instead of turning to face the tunnel entrance to the road, started to rise upwards.

"Activate the sky-entrance AMIe" said Adam as the car continued to rise.

"Sky-Entrance?" Mate queried and Adam had only laughed in reply.

At the rear of Jupiter house, there was a large decked patio area with sun loungers, outside seating and b-b-q areas. Suddenly, all the furniture moved to the side as if by magic, as the central area with its two-tiered layout, lifted upwards, like a shield between the opening and the expanse of glass windows, just as the i8 emerged through the dark and up into the sky, carried on new underfloor jets that gave it a new vertical lift-off capability.

Once clear of the opened decking, the car ignited its rear jets and was quickly no more than a dot on the distant landscape, leaving the decking to reset itself as the open portion lowered into position and the furniture returned to its previous places.

"That was amazing" exclaimed Mate. "How long have you been keeping that a secret?".

Adam smiled back "A while. This version of the i8 has been my little pet project for some time and only the destruction of the previous car hastened this one on".

"And the decking?"

"Oh that was always there. I figured one day I might need a quick or alternative access into the caves below, so I had different contractors working on different aspects of the mechanism and completed the installation myself. Now, lets go get Wednesday!".

At the laboratory, Heather could hear the two men throwing chairs and equipment about in their rage at not being able to find the Dr. She was just wondering if the alarm had worked when the screen on the watch flashed a message 'go to the roof'.

The staircase for the last two storeys was separate to the one she'd been hiding on, and she quickly took the steps two at a time, before bursting out onto the roof. Bolting the door behind her she scanned the roof area but there was no-one there. Thinking she'd been mis-directed or tricked even, she turned to unbolt the door when the wind suddenly rose around her and turning, whilst shielding her eyes with a raised hand, she saw the car setting down on the roof and the door opening. Adam was waving at her urgently to get in.

As they'd approached the laboratory complex where AMIe had identified Wednesday's alarm as coming from, Adam turned to Mate and suggested that he dissipate and check out Wednesday's laboratory room. You could almost see Mate grin as slowly the suit deflated and Mate dissolved through the seat and floor of the car in flight, and headed for the bright lights of the 4th floor.

He passed easily through the wall and was able to 'see' the two men, wreaking havoc on the rooms furnishings and equipment. Time to teach these two bullies a lesson he thought as he approached one of them from behind, so he picked up a long-legged stool and swung it towards the unsuspecting hoodlum.

With a crash, it sent the bewildered man flying across the room, slamming him into the opposite wall and rendering him unconscious. Oops, he really must try and remember that his strength had increased many fold in this molecular form.

Now the remaining bandit, realising that something was up, decided to abandon the building as he headed for the lifts.

He reached the bank of elevators and was pressing the call button with ever more urgency as the furniture in the room kept throwing itself about, the destruction leaving the room as a table and stool began swirling in mid-air, heading towards him.

At the last possible minute, the lift doors opened and the terrified man sprung in, shutting the doors quickly behind him, and pressing the 'Ground' button,

Slumping against the back wall, the man wiped his hands over his face, thankful for his lucky escape.

Suddenly the lift lurched and stopped, the floor indicators showing he was trapped between the 2nd and 3rd floors.

The lift lights flickered momentarily and then to the man's relief burned brightly once more. The next thing, and the man screamed out in terror as the lift began a deathly unchecked plunge towards the basement.

In the lift shaft, the end of the cable normally attached to the lift roof swung motionless before beginning a lazy looping movement. Like someone preparing to throw a lasso.

Outside, Adam was already navigating the car away, back towards his home, before Wednesday had even a chance to speak. "Thank you" she managed.

"You're welcome" replied Adam, not taking his eyes from the way ahead.

"Are you OK?".

"Just a little shook up" she replied. "Those men would have killed me if they'd found me. It was blind luck that I'd taken a break and gone to the floor above to use the kitchen area".

"I'm afraid the attack might have been my fault" replied Adam as he told her about his earlier visit to see Winston Tek and the discussion they'd had.

When he'd finished recounting the days earlier events, she turned to him and said "So Tek is the one behind this attempt on my life".

"I'm afraid so and I think it's probably safer if you stay with me for a while. C'mom, we'll stop by your home and you can collect some things".

The next day dawned sunny and bright with a slight haze on the distant horizon. It was going to be another fine day and already, farmers were preparing their machinery to head out into the fields of corn and hay.

Wednesday woke and took a minute to remember where she was. The terrifying attempt on her life the night before and the escape thanks to Adam and his incredible tech, before his offer to her to continue her work in the safety and security of his own home.

AMIe finished drawing back the blinds to reveal the full panorama and wished the Dr "Good morning". "You'll find breakfast is ready in the dining room and Adam already there".

Wednesday thanked AMIe and headed for the en-suite shower. After a brief refreshing wash in the tropical shower, with all its modern settings for power, type of pattern and massaging jets, she changed into casual top and jeans and walked barefoot through the house to breakfast.

Adam was already sat at one end of the table, with a small digital pad, flicking the screen upwards. An empty plate with just a few toast crumbs left, and a large white coffee cup sat just to his right.

He was just reaching, without taking his eyes from the pad, for the coffee as Wednesday entered.

Instantly putting the pad down, he rose with a smile and asked her if she'd slept well?

"Yes thank you. I think that's the softest, most comfortable bed I've ever slept in".

"Coffee" asked Adam reaching for the sideboard, to which she nodded and helping herself to toast, sat looking out of the window, with its view towards Cambridge in the shimmering distance.

"I really can't thank you enough" she began, "for putting me up like this and the use of your equipment to continue my work".

"It's the very least I can do. It's my fault those hoodlums attached you last night, and destroyed your own facility in the process".

"AMIe has already downloaded all your work into the systems here and I've set up a computer and screens ready for you, whenever you're ready".

"What happened to the two men?. Will they come after me again?".

"No, you're quite safe. My friend and colleague took care of them, as we made our escape".

"You left him behind?" She asked disbelievingly.

"Not exactly" replied Adam. "Mate had his own means of transport".

Adam led Wednesday to the fountain and before touching the hand rail, pointed out that he'd programmed her biometrics into the house's security system. "For what?" She replied.

"For this" smiled Adam as he reached out and touched the rail.

Instantly, the fountain transformed into the hidden entranceway it concealed, and before Wednesday had time to marvel at the transformation, like some magicians sliding mirror trick, she was across the small walkway that had appeared out of the pond, and was joining Adam in the rather compact lift.

As soon as the lift doors closed, it moved downward in an exhilarating rush, before coming to a controlled halt seconds later.

Wondering what she was going to see, the doors opened to reveal the short chalky tunnel which entered out into a more comfy area of workshops and laboratories,

Adam guided her into the nearest room, all white, seamless, and equipped with large computer screens and banks of monitors and other robotic equipment. She was still barefoot and looked down to the tiled floor, that wasn't at all cold. Adam noticed her look and said "underfloor heating keeps a constant, comfortable temperature in most parts of the 'Lab".

"Here's your work station. AMIe is voice activated and can assist with any cross-referencing, data analysis or enquiry. AMIe, why don't you give the Dr a brief demonstration".

"I'd be delighted to" replied AMIe, in her usual soft voice and straight away, large monitors overhanging Wednesday's work desk came to life, one showing a map representation of her buoys with a live data stream from each buoy appearing on a second monitor.

A third was showing a representation of the the Polestarr data, both as it was reporting and a separate reading calibrated to the adjustments they'd recorded upon inspecting the satellite up close.

Her Mac screen had also come to life and a small black pad to the right of the keyboard flashed a blinking, single blue led.

"Please place your thumb or preferred finger on the bio-metric plate. This will enable you to switch from any workstation and is also your secure login".

Wednesday placed her thumb to the plate and instantly, the Mac computer screen came to life.

"This is incredible" stammered Wednesday to Adam, lost for words.

"I'm glad you approve" replied Adam. His watch bleeped twice and turning his wrist to look at the face, which had illuminated briefly, said "C'mon, Mate should be waiting for us".

She followed him into a separate smaller room, this one with more comfortable furnishings and several large sofa's, upon which one laid what looked like an all in one work-suit layer, out as though ready for someone to change into.

Price: Polestarr

Taking a seat in the opposite armchair, she'd barely sat down, when the suit started to fill out, like someone was pumping up an inflatable.

As the suit filled out, so she noticed that the suit was completely enclosed and where there would have been holes at the end of sleeves and legs, were sewn in gloves and trainer-boots. Even the face was covered with a black mesh, a high collar hiding most of the facial area, and a hood covering the back of the head & neck.

The suit had finished filling out and now it stood upright in front of her as a man's voice said pleasantly, "Hello Dr Week. It's good to see you again".

Wednesday, pausing only to catch her breath, replied almost automatically, whilst turning to Adam with a puzzled look.

"I'm Mate" continued the suit. "Adam's friend and colleague, we met before but I was already fully suited then", holding out a gloved hand to shake Wednesday's, which she took, not quite believing what she'd seen.

"Excuse me but are you a real person inside there?"

"Yes" replied Mate, and although the suit lacked the ability to convert facial expressions, you got the impression the last had been said with a broad smile.

"Mate suffered accidental exposure to a concoction based on my fusion reactor's stabilising fluid - the stuff that makes the whole thing work, in our last adventure. Somehow, and for reasons we're still exploring, it altered Mate into a bio-chemical collection of particles, that he can concentrate and control into an almost physical presence.

I developed the suit to help him concentrate those particles. The concentrating takes an enormous amount of effort and drains Mate's capability to remain 'whole' for any period of time. The suit gives him roughly 8 to 10 hours in any 20 hour period, before he quite literally dissolves. We just witnessed the re-animation process".

"And for my next trick" said Mate, who during Adam's explanation had been wandering about the room.

"Party pieces can wait" said Adam patiently. "Right now, we all have work to do" and leaving a still partly open-mouthed Wednesday with Mate, walked back to the main laboratory area.

Chapter 7

7. The Vandenberg Appointment.

Adam had accepted 'Tek's invitation to tour his facility in the States, and had been working on a number of covert devices that would hopefully let them access Tek Corps systems. It was too good an opportunity to miss, and as he got ready for his encounter, so Mate and Wednesday helped with programming and other bits of background information, and the questions to ask.

Adam had decided the journey was too dangerous to take Wednesday on, and because Mate would be invaluable in penetrating those areas of Tek's HQ undetected, was timing their departure to give Mate as much time as possible in his concentrated form.

That same evening, everything ready for a departure the following morning, Adam and Wednesday were relaxing with a glass of wine, having finished a delicious late supper prepared by AMIe, with Adam's help.

The doorbell rang and AMIe announced that Heather was at the door. "Please let her in" requested Adam, as Wednesday heard the door open and quick footsteps on the tiled floor announcing her friend Heather's arrival.

Taking the proffered glass of wine, and taking an appreciative sip, she sat down on the same sofa as Wednesday, and with a slight glint to her eye, asked her how she was enjoying her stay.

Wednesday had gushed with the description of the working facilities, the kindness of Adam, and touched briefly on her rescue. She started to talk about Mate when she stopped herself. Perhaps it wasn't common knowledge? "It's OK said Heather, I know all about Mate. I was there with Adam when it happened. It's really my fault. He threw himself in front of the burst liquid container, and saved me".

"I've asked Heather to come and stay a few days with us, so you'll have some company, and hopefully feel a little safer, whilst Mate and I are in America".

"You're going then?" Queried Heather.

"Yes, I can't miss the opportunity to get inside his organisation and try and learn what he's really up to".

"I have some information of my own", said Heather, reaching for her satchel bag. Opening the
82

flap and pulling a sheaf of papers from one of the dividers, she passed them to Adam. "A contact in the anti-terrorist unit intercepted an unusual radio signal, similar to a mobile phone, but almost hidden in the noise of the usual mobile traffic. He wasn't able to recover the call itself but was able to locate where the call went to".

"And?" Replied Adam, continuing to look at the data on the sheets in front of him.

"It originated from Vandenberg, America. It suggests a link between The Children of WAW and Winston Tek, or at least his organisation, but what I don't understand is why would someone like Winston Tek get involved with climate protestors?. It just doesn't make sense".

"Well, hopefully, that's something you and Wednesday can work on while I'm in America. Now it's late and I suggest we all get some rest".

"I've made up one of the Guest rooms ready for you Ms Lightly" spoke AMIe, and with that, the three of them rose and AMIe turned down the lights and closed the curtains.

Another fine day! They really were being blessed with some beautiful weather in the South of England;

indeed much of the UK, as Adam finished loading his bags into the rear of the i8.

Mate was just re-animating in the adjoining room, as Adam said goodbye to Wednesday & Heather. "Be on your guard. It's highly likely that Winston Tek may send some of his goons here, whilst he knows I'm away in his company. AMIe has been briefed and is taking care of all the security arrangements".

Mate had now joined them, and he and Adam climbed into the bronze i8 car, gleaming under the lights of the garage as the tunnel door opened and they drove out to the surface.

Once on that stretch of track that had once been the old private railway of a steam enthusiast, Adam applied more power and extending the delta-wings built into the under-skirts of the car, took to the air, in a steep arcing climb.

Even though Vandenberg was located on the Californian West Coast of America, the flight still took under two-hours, during which time the pair talked about the mission ahead and offered hypothesis on the connection with the violence at the climate protests. What could it all mean? was a question with which they busied themselves during the short flight, AMIe at the helm of the auto-pilot until the West Coast came into view.

Price: Polestarr

Adam had already located a suitably quiet road on which to land at, and taking manual control tilted the car towards the stretch of desert highway he'd chosen.

Touching down on the well-maintained road, that disappeared into the already present heat-haze of the early Californian morning, that ran into Lompoc, a nearby town to Vandenberg, they drove onto their hotel, where Adam was expected.

Pulling into the car park, Adam got out and surveyed the hotel's frontage. Large and impressive with the suggestion that only well-to-do people should consider staying there. Whilst the thought was disdainful to Adam, it was only the fact that it was the only hotel with any spare rooms, the rest of the hotels and motels being fully booked by space enthusiasts ahead of another launch planned for tomorrow from the old Air Force base nearby.

Mate had already dissipated and followed Adam into the hotel only to learn which room number they were in.

The formalities of checking in completed, the rather stern looking receptionist had called to a nearby bell-boy to collect Adam's luggage and show him suite 301.

They followed the young man across the marbled reception area, with its decorative columns and soft lighting to a gilded lift, which took them to the third floor ("reserved exclusively for suites") and were escorted to the far end of the corridor, before being let into a light & airy apartment, which consisted of a bedroom and separate lounge area.

The large French door style windows were open, allowing a pleasant breeze to blow in, billowing the curtains as it did. Adam went to the first open door to admire the view out across the town to the ocean far in the distance.

"Can you watch the launches from here?" He asked.

"Yes sir came the eager reply. If you follow the line of sight just to the right, you'll get a fine view, and on still days, the sound of the rockets is quite something, even at this distance. Well enjoy your stay sir" the last said as he gratefully pocketed the tip Adam had passed to him.

His meeting with Tek wasn't until the afternoon, so Adam set about unpacking his few things amongst which was a second, thinner all-in-one suit for Mate, which he laid out on the palatial sized bed.

Price: Polestarr

Instantly it began filling out as Mate re-emerged and once full, the small transmitter sewn into the collar blinked green as Mate stood up and walked about the room, "Very nice".

"Hmm, a pity you can't experience all the amenities" replied Adam, helping himself to a lime tonic from the well stocked fridge in the corner of the room.

"Oh you mean that charming receptionist".

"You were there?" Asked Adam.

"I saw the whole thing. She nearly threw the room keys at you when you said you were only staying the one night".

"No hotel likes tying up a room for a single night. The missed opportunity to sell a several night stay instead, particularly during launch season".

"I'm going to shower and change ready for my meeting with Tek. See you back in the car".

Changed & refreshed, Adam wasted no time in walking back outside to the car and climbing in.

AMIe confirmed Mate was in the car, just not in his suit, for the drive out to Tek's complex at the former Air Force base, as Adam pulled out onto the quiet road.

Arriving at Vandenberg, an armed security patrol stopped the car at a gated barrier. Adam lowered the driver's window and smiled pleasantly at the approaching guard, who did not return the smile, but instead shifted the large automatic rifle in his hands.

"Name and business please?" "I'm Dr Adam Price, here by invitation to visit Mr Winston Tek".

At the mention of Tek's name, the guards whole manner changed, to one of the utmost helpfulness and politeness. The rifle was instantly slung back over the shoulder as the guard motioned for the gate to be opened immediately, saying as Adam pulled away, "Welcome to Vandenberg".

Whistling to himself through clenched teeth at the site of the gleaming BMW as it pulled away, his colleague immediately questioned why he'd suddenly let the visitor through so quickly? "That limey was here to visit Winston Tek - by invitation no less". The second guard could only convey his amazement at what his friend had told him, by pushing his helmet back over his forehead and scratching it perplexedly.

Adam followed the invitation's brief instructions to find the Tek building but it was hardly necessary.

They stood tall and imposing above any other building around. Tel Corp was written in letters a meter high across the front of the building that seemed built of entirely polished black glass.

Tasteful raised borders of exotic plants and flowers bordered the sweeping pathway up to the entrance doors where a secretary waited patiently as Adam got out of the car and taking a jacket from a small hook behind the drivers seat, walked easily towards her.

"Welcome to the Tek Corp headquarters" she recited. "My name is Anita and I'm here to make your visit as comfortable as possible. It's so nice to welcome you again Dr Price. May I offer you some refreshment?".

"No, nothing for me thank you" replied Adam, as Anita led him up a small flight of stairs and off to the left of the main elevator doors to a smaller lift.

Inserting a key taken from a small chain on her skirt, the lift doors opened and admitted them both. The quick ascent was without conversation, and when the lift stopped with a soft ping, Anita didn't exit the lift but merely waved her arm indicating that Adam should step out. "Mr Tek will be with you momentarily", and she was gone as the private lift doors slid shut.

"Welcome Dr Price" The voice and the manner were completely unchanged from their last encounter. Winston seemed even more at ease in his own surroundings than he had been in London. Despite the large gestures, not a movement was wasted, not a syllable uttered unnecessarily as Tek swooped down from a raised dais to greet Adam.

"It's very good of you to receive me so soon after your invitation. Business necessitated by being in Los Angeles and the nearness to you, made it too good an opportunity to miss. That and a launch scheduled for tomorrow. I've never seen a real rocket launch up close before".

"That's just swell. I'd be delighted if you'd share my personal viewing rooms at the mission control tomorrow. It promises to be quite a show".

"Now how may I be of assistance? I understand from discreet enquiries that you're a noted man of science yourself and are still labouring on a new fusion reactor energy source, is that correct?".

And so Adam and Tek had talked about research, the problems associated with funding such work and the importance it could play on the Global Warming stage, at length.

Meanwhile, Mate had passed through the reception are unnoticed and was already exploring the off-limits areas to visitors.

After drifting through several offices and meeting rooms, he came to another meeting room, with a more austere look to it that the others. A projector was set up and loaded with slides whilst another was linked to a small computer terminal, designed for a laptop to snap into.

Turning his attention to the slides, he focused, concentrating his whole core and mind into forming the index finger of his right hand. Slowly the finger took shape, the air around it distorting and a small globe with a faint blue tinge also appearing at the base of the second knuckle.

He concentrated still further until the spectral finger took on an even more solid appearance, before moving to the projector and flicking the 'on' switch.

The projector came noisily to life, the carousel clattering and the slide shutter moving back and forth as each slide was presented on the far wall.

The images were of a region of one of the Poles. There were others of drilling and mining equipment designed specifically for operating in freezing temperatures followed by detailed cost and time-frames for some exploration exercise.

The final slide showed an architect blueprint for a structure, that looked half-buried inside a mountain, although it was difficult to tell as the drawing was a cut-away, half segment view. Some ecologically advanced house perhaps?

There was noise in the corridor and Mate quickly dissolved his finger and passed back through the wall he'd come from.

The door opened and Anita, the secretary that had greeted Adam at the entrance walked into the room. She stopped at the projector and frowning, turned it off, removing the slides and pocketing them into the small shoulder bag she carried.

Checking again the room was empty, she left, the lock turning with a click, indicating she'd secured the door from the other side.

Tek was showing Adam some plans of the power-plants he'd used in his Polestarr satellite programme when the phone console on his desk beeped once. Excusing himself, he took his desk seat and picked up the receiver.

Although Adam strained to hear what was being said, he was only able to make out the words "access" and "empty room". The voice on the other end was female.

At the end of the short conversation, Tek had only grunted before replacing the receiver, and once again, flashing that large smile of his, approached Adam and said "say, you're here for the launch tomorrow. Why don't we drive out to the launchpad now and you can get a proper close-up look. Give me a minute to make all the arrangements and I'll have my driver meet us out front".

Adam thanked him for the opportunity and while Tek made the call, recovered his jacket from the nearby chair, as Tek motioned him to follow him downstairs.

As the car was waved through the final barrier, Tek became the consummate tour guide, pointing out the sights of former launches, their historical importance and the missions that had launched from them.

Space travel had still seemed very science fiction but men like him, with vision and means, had dragged this country into the space age, winning the ultimate race to the Moon.

Now the launch gantry was becoming suddenly much larger than life as it towered above the block buildings they passed and the water tower adjacent to the launch pad.

The car slewed around and came to a stop short of one of the smaller block buildings. Both men got out of the car, and stood, hands shielding their eyes as each tipped their heads back to take in the faraway tip of the rocket, white and gleaming, with thin wispy vapour trails of escaping fuel.

"This way Dr Price" motioned Tek, "I think you'll find the water delivery system that deadens the shock waves of launch particularly interesting. Adam noticed that the driver / security guard also followed them, as Tek took a key from his pocket and inserting it carefully into a lock on the small door, opened it and led the party in and down a flight of steel steps.

They came out into a concrete walled pit. In each direction, North, East, South & West ran large slanted viaducts, whilst above them, the opening was directly beneath the powerful rockets themselves.

This close they looked enormous and Adam wondered at the structure around them being able to contain the fiery power the three engines could deliver.

Tek must have read his mind as he came up to him and nodding, said "Yes sir the power feeding through those propulsion systems is incredible. More incredible is this structure that delivers enough water to fill a small reservoir in minutes. Water is fed from those mushroom shaped delivery points above, starting momentarily before the rockets themselves ignite, the exhaust is channeled down these four exit points" pointing to the four viaducts as he spoke.

"You will feel the ground shake under you. It's a sensation you can't forget in a hurry, but is equally exhilarating every time you experience it.".

Adam turned and was just saying how much he was looking forward to the launch when Tek cut him off by finishing "unfortunately for you Dr Price, it is an experience you will only get to witness once". As Adam slumped to the floor, the security guard withdrew the small syringe needle from Adam's neck and said "Like that?".

"Yes" replied Tek, "Just like that".

Jonathan C. Crouch

Chapter 8

8. Tek's Trap.

Mate had finished his surveillance of the Tek offices and finding nothing else of interest, had floated back to the hotel, to wait for Adam as arranged.

It was only some hours later, as it was beginning to grow dark that Mate became worried. There had been no word from Adam and he hadn't returned to the hotel. It was possible he was taking a look at some area or building from the i8 but unlikely.

He contacted Heather and Wednesday and shared his concerns, and AMIe was working on getting a location fix on Adam, when suddenly Mate started dissipating. 'Oh no not now" he just had time to mumble before the suit went flat and Mate was gone.

"Mate, Mate" cried Heather into the microphone but there was no reply. Only tantalising static. Wednesday placed a hand on her arm and said "He's gone. Come, we have to work on this together. You know how Adam's mind works. What is likely to have happened to him?

AMIe, are you able to get any location fix on Adam?"

"Nothing" replied AMIe solemnly, "The car is still parked at the Tek Offices. My surveillance recorded Adam and Winston Tek being chauffeur driven away earlier in their afternoon. The car was spotted on the CCTV heading towards launch control. Neither Adam, Tek or the car have returned".

Heather swung the seat around and looked earnestly at Wednesday. "I have contacts, old contacts of Adam's in the security services, but I'm not sure if this warrants calling them"

"You mean that rather dashing old gentleman?. Yes I've met him and he was most insistent that his department were not at Adam's beck and call".

"For now, it's just up to us", and the pair of them sat down to respective computers and began punching their keyboards as they searched for Adam.

Winston Tek was already boarding his private jet, when Mission Control messaged him to say the launch was proceeding as planned and no delays were expected. "Yes, he murmured to himself. Exactly as planned".

98

Price: Polestarr

As the jet took off and the under-carriage retracted, he looked out of the adjacent window towards the Vandenberg complex shoreline. A pity he wouldn't be there to watch the launch in person.

Perhaps it was the jets engines, or some other aircraft passing overhead nearby, before the air space became restricted ahead of the launch, that finally roused Adam from his drug-induced sleep.

The air was already dry, indicating that the early morning had passed. His eyes came into focus and he found himself staring straight up at the three rockets he'd marvelled at earlier.

He tried to move from his laying position and discovered his torso, arms, legs and feet were bound tightly. The rope that had been used trailed away to an iron ring set in the floor of the concrete less than a meter away. The proverbial tethered goat he mused to himself.

He lay back, forcing himself to concentrate and calm down with breathing techniques, while his mind pondered the immediate problem before him.

In Mission Control, the clock had stopped at T minus 10 minutes as part of a scheduled break in the countdown, during which final checks were completed and any fuel topping up was attended to.

Ground crews had already evacuated the area and the launch pad controller had given a 'GO' for launch.

In 5 minutes time, the countdown would resume.

Adam had been wriggling his hands and wrists trying to loosen the heavy rope and knots to no avail. He was trussed like a Thanksgiving turkey and was soon going to be as crispy as chicken wings unless he came up with something and fast. Judging by the position of the shadows the Sun was casting, it couldn't be long until launch.

Mechanical sounding bumps came from the rocket machinery hanging above him. Fuel pumps! The countdown must be in the last few minutes if they'd started up.

Frantically he looked about for something anything he could use to help free him. Kobayashi Maru! There really was no way out of this one.

Back at Jupiter House, Heather and Wednesday had worked through the night trying to locate Adam with no success. The usual tracking devices they all carried were not working or being blocked by something.

Heather rubbed her eyes, and was reaching for another coffee when a familiar static began filling the loudspeakers as Mate's voice finally became coherent once again.

"Any luck tracing Adam?" Asked Mate. "None" replied Heather and Wednesday in unison.

"What about his transponder signal?"

"Either blocked or not working" replied Wednesday. "Assuming the equipment hasn't malfunctioned, then the only thing that could be blocking the signal is an anti-magnetic suppression, but that's really old science, developed by NASA".

"What was it used for specifically?" Asked Mate, a distinctly unpleasant thought growing in his mind.

"It was used to suppress magnetic interference of rocket launches, like anti-magnetic tools, but this was more to do with the rocket guidance and anti-toppling effects".

"There's a launch planned today" stated Heather. "You don't think.." The sentence trailed off as Mate dissipated and was already heading for the Vandenberg base as fast as he could.

The countdown pre-flight checks were complete and one by one, the individual stations in Mission Control had give a "Go for flight", as the 10 minute countdown resumed.

Laying in the launch tower exhaust pit, Adam had managed to free one frozen, numb hand and was starting on the knots tied around his feet without success.

Above him the rocket structure groaned and gurgled as the behemoth started coming to life, before it was catapulted to the stars.

Mate was only vaguely aware of his surroundings as he 'flew' in his dissipated form. He sensed rather than saw, the launchpad approaching as he swooped around the tall rocket looking for any signs of Adam.

The few remaining minutes ticked by.

A glint, like sunlight catching jewellery suddenly caught his eye, and Mate quickly transferred down to the ground. Looking over into the pit below he could see Adam bound and struggling to free himself.

Mate dropped and was beside Adam in an instant as he began re-forming himself enough to be of help.

Adam realised his old friend was there and said instantly "You've got to get away. There's less than minutes before launch".

"And leave you?" Replied Mate, "not a chance. Although I'm having no luck with these knots".

Suddenly, Adam remembered the tour Tek had given him and the small block they'd passed through to access the steel stairwell to the launch pit.

"There's an emergency abort button in the small room above us. It's there for the pad crew to use in case of a fire or fuel leak. Pressing it should alert Mission Control & stop the launch. Hurry, we barely have a minute left".

Mate immediately dissipated and passed upwards through the concrete floor into the room above. Seeing the abort button attached to a nearby pillar, he used all his concentration to reform a finger & press the small red button.

The Flight Director leant forward, standing at his desk, as the countdown clock reached 10 seconds, 9, 8, Main Engine start.. suddenly a large 'ABORT' message flashed up on the main Mission Control screens as computers scrabbled to shut down the big engines before they could ignite, and mission controllers looked at each other in wonderment.

Mate floated back down to Adam and sat with him in a partially formed state, while they waited for help to arrive, as approaching sirens could already be heard in the distance.

In Mission Control. The Flight Director looked at the screen which held the countdown clock, steadfast at T minus 5 seconds.

The silver fire-suited fireman had found Adam still partially tied up in the launch pit, and after using bolt cutters to free him, had carried him to a waiting ambulance, where he was declared fit, if not a little hydrated. With no long lasting ill-effects likely, the ambulance crew closed the vans doors and headed for the small, private hospital on the Base's grounds.

"The Medic riding with Adam in the back of the ambulance was speaking as the van bumped along the concourse roads at speed. "You're lucky to be alive. The countdown was stopped at 5 seconds to go. Something triggered the Abort, which was lucky for you. Say, what were you doing down there anyway?".

"You should know better than to ask questions like that" replied Adam smiling for the first time since his rescue. "I do need to make a phone call though - there will be people worried about me".

"Here, use my mobile" said the Medic, handing Adam the small rectangular device. Adam quickly dialled the number for Jupiter House, which AMIe would re-route to where-ever Heather and Wednesday were.

After two rings, the phone was answered by a breathless Heather, who'd jumped from her stool, rousing a sleepy Wednesday as she'd run to the landline phone on the other desk.

"It's Adam" she cried excitedly to Wednesday's enquiring look.

Adam kept the conversation short, not wanting to give too much away in front of the Medic, but assured Heather he was well and safe now. "I'll call later once the Medics have finished with me, and I should be on a flight home later.

However, it wasn't until the next day that Adam was allowed to leave the small field hospital. The doctors were concerned for his dehydration and the blood analysis had revealed a potent knock-out drug in his system, and they wanted to make sure that all traces were gone.

Also, the base authorities wanted to know what he was doing there, and it was only after a call from some of Adam's friends at Langley that the agents withdrew without any further questions.

Adam had slept fitfully, his mind playing over the events of the past 24 hours and picking at the threads of deceit carefully, trying to decipher the meaning behind it all. So many times he picked a promising strand only to follow it to a dead-end.

The medical monitors attached to him recorded periods of intense brain activity before the mind quieted and Adam slept soundly.

The following morning, the young Doctor who'd been in charge of his treatment the day before, paid a visit to the patient, and after asking how Adam felt and reviewing the charts hanging on a nearby wall bracket, pronounced Adam fit to leave.

Adam thanked him and his staff for their care and as he was getting dressed so the Doctor returned quickly with a message that a Dr Week was waiting for him in the reception, come to take him home.

Adam checked his appearance in the full length mirror on the back of the small hospital wardrobe door, and apart from a few scuffs on his face, where he'd fought to free himself, he looked almost rosy-cheeked.

Stopping only to thank the nurses, sat at the monitoring station, he walked down the corridor to the reception, where Wednesday was sitting waiting for him.

As he entered the area, so she jumped up and ran to him, catching him in a tight hug of joy at his being alive & well.

"Steady" he said, separating from the embrace, "I may be fragile". She stepped back, catching her breath and sweeping her hair out of her face, said with a little more composure, "I'm sorry. It's just so good to see you alive and unharmed. We were quite frantic when we couldn't locate you and it was only thanks to Mate's timely return that the missing piece of the puzzle was added and gave us an idea of where to look".

"And not a moment too soon" replied Adam smiling.

"The cars parked outside, after I collected it from outside Tek's offices. The man himself hasn't returned".

"Nor is he likely too" replied Adam. "He'll know I'm onto him and the authorities will also want a quiet word I daresay. No, he'll have gone to ground, but where?".

As they both climbed into the patiently waiting i8, so AMIe expressed her gratefulness that Adam was alive & well, before saying that she'd been tracking all movements without success of finding Tek.

"He has enough money, influence and power to disappear if he wants too but I suspect it won't be too long before we hear from him again" said Adam, more to himself than Wednesday & AMIe.

Initiating drive mode, they drove off the base and were soon on a quiet, deserted stretch of road before Adam engaged the flight mode, and applied a little too much power as Wednesday was thrown back into her seat and the i8 soared up into the morning sky.

Chapter 9

9. The Spy Trawler.

Adam had flown as hard and fast as he dared, and already less than two hours later, the English coast was a faint outline out of the windscreen.

The brief flight had given them both plenty of time to knock about theories in what Tek was really up to, and although none of the hypothesis were completely satisfactory, it had concentrated their minds on several key questions, the answers to which, could just provide the breakthrough answer they sought.

"The only thing we know for certain is the data manipulation. The question still remains why would anyone want the World to think it was cooler than it actually was?" Wednesday had finally mused.

"I've been giving that a lot of thought", replied Adam. "What would be the consequences of the the the World's governments relaxing of the emissions, if they thought the didn't have to be quite so stringent to meet pre-determined targets, based on old data?".

"I suppose they would go back to their old ways of mining and using fossil fuels". "Third-World and developing countries would breathe the biggest sigh of relief because their efforts would be less hampered to develop economically".

"And which area or region is most at risk and faced the heaviest sanctions on mining and development?" Replied Adam.

"Well there are several key areas" replied Wednesday. "The rain forests of South America. The Artic and Antarctic regions and of course, the Oceans".

"And Tek is hiding out in one of those areas" said Adam matter-of-factly, "we just have to figure out which one".

Now the English countryside was taking on a more familiar pattern of fields, hedgerows and roads, with clusters of houses scattered about, as the i8 dropped height and approached that sleepy little corner of Cambridgeshire, where Adam lived. AMIe had already scanned the nearby roads and selected one that was straight and devoid of traffic for a more conventional landing, as Adam took the controls and handled the transition from air to road with the faintest of bumps, as the car's tyres made contact with the single track road, lined with birch and horse chestnut trees.

110

Minutes later and they were at the old deserted farm building, which held the hidden ramp entrance to Adam's underground base, as the ground swallowed the car and its occupants up, before resetting itself and re-camouflaging the dusty floor to its original untouched state of appearance.

As the car pulled up in the garage area so Heather was already there to welcome them both back.

"Mate's halfway through his dissipated cycle" she said in reply to Adam's querying look for his friend.

The three of them walked into the main laboratory room and positioning themselves around a circular table that had an overhead projection system fitted, Adam spoke "AMIe, bring up the 3D modelling project I've been working on and show us the whole world". The table came to life as laser beams criss-crossed the area, and slowly a three dimensional outline of the World appeared, spinning slowly.

"Now highlight those areas most heavily protected by current climate legislation, not matter how small". Areas of the land mass started filling in, whilst areas of the oceans also did the same.

Some areas were a deeper colour than others and AMIe explained the deeper shades meant the area was more highly protected.

As Adam has surmised on the journey, South America and the two Poles were the areas most at risk.

"AMIe, has there been any unusual activity in any of these regions in the last six months?" Queried Adam.

"Where are you going with this?" Asked Wednesday.

"I have a hunch" replied Adam, hoping he was wrong.

AMIe had taken several minutes to work on Adam's last enquiry, when she finally spoke and said "I might have something". "I'll make the data appear on the adjacent screens". As she spoke, so the screens started coming to life with flashing, over-lapping images of official looking documents, purchase orders and satellite images of ground movements.

"Taken at face value, none of these events or documents seem linked in anyway, however, if you factor in what's missing, i.e. the relaxing of mining rights, then suddenly a tenuous link does appear".

"Show me" replied Adam.

"Documents for land purchase spread over several different solicitors under the names of different

112

companies. If you follow them far enough back, they are all owned by Tek Corp.

Combine the land they pertain the purchase to, and you get this". The 3-D globe outline sound and zoomed in on the Artic region. As shapes of land started to colour in, it quickly became apparent that Tek had purchased a sizeable chunk of land mass.

"Before Christmas, the area was quiet" began AMIe, "but in January, less than two months after the final land deal was completed, we see a lot of movement on the surface, near this particular mountain range".

They looked at the satellite imagery, which showed snow vehicles, trucks and sleds moving about the area, their tracks leaving deep imprints on the snowy surface.

Buildings began to appear and mining equipment, before the activity quieted down and the trucks and sleds retreated they way the'd come, towards an area that had been turned into small airport.

On one of the images, a large transport plane could be seen leaving the end of the runway.

Adam zoomed out of the map, using hand gestures and pinching movements, until they could see the nearby coastline.

Save for icebergs, the area was devoid save for a handful of fishing trawlers in the various images.

Whilst they'd come and gone, like ants walking on a map, only one had remained roughly in the same position. Engine trouble? Unlikely. What's more, the other trawlers had given it a wide berth.

"If I didn't know better.." Began Adam, before suddenly wheeling round and walking quickly towards the garage.

"Where are you going?" Shouted Heather after him.

"To see an old friend" came the reply, as the familiar whine of the car's power plant started up and burst up the exit tunnel.

It was falling dusk by the time Adam had made the short journey into London and was pulling up at the barrier entrance to a familiar old Multi-storey car park.

The barrier lifted as he approached, a single, seemingly old and dilapidated CCTV camera pivoted following the cars entrance into the car park before returning to its original position. As the car drove downwards towards the farthest basement level, so more old, rusty cameras followed its patch, until the car came to a stop in a space marked reserved, written in crumbling, fading yellow letters.

Adam sat in the car, considering his next move. He'd been warned about approaching his old employers again, and whilst their surveillance techniques were not as sophisticated as his own, they were effective nonetheless.

Suddenly, without warning, the floor area the car was parked in began to descend. The decision obviously being made for him, Adam sat patiently in the car as the huge lift slowly descended through layers of tarmac and concrete then poured concrete as finally it emerged into a large hall, lit by a single spotlight.

The car elevator came to a stop, and Adam stepped out of the car onto the bare concrete floor. Nearby, a small tube train platform stood silent, with no train waiting. Turning back towards the source of the single spotlight, he looked up at the ceiling to see the hole the car had travelled through, close up. The second the last millimetre was closed, the whole room was flooded with light, and Adam had to quickly adjust his eyesight to a squint.

A figure in outline, back lit by the bright lights, was walking patiently towards him, a familiar walking cane in one hand, as the shadowy figure's face was caught

115

in the light and Adam found himself looking upon the rather stern face of his old boss and friend.

"What may I ask, brings you calling again so soon. I'd have thought our last meeting was enough to dissuade you from making frivolous contact". Despite the severity of the reproof, it had been uttered with just the merest hint of a smile. The pale eyes unblinking, stern.

"It's nice to see you too" replied Adam returning the upward slant of one corner of his mouth. "I think I might have stumbled upon some information concerning the whereabouts of Winston Tek and.. " he paused for effect, "one of your spy trawlers".

Seated in the old gent's office, Adam lost no time in re-counting all the information they's gleaned from the multi-layered analysis of the Artic region, secretly purchased by Tek. It was when they were cross-referencing the data and widened the scope of the surveillance of the activity that the trawler, which definitely wasn't fishing, had become apparent to them.

"And if its apparent to me then you can be sure that other parties, namely Winston Tek, will have noticed it as well. For their own safety, get those men out of their now".

116

The old gent had said nothing during Adam's explanation; just sat there hands closed fingers to fingers in silent contemplation. Only when Adam had mentioned the spy trawler had he leaned forward a little, unfurling his hands and placing them squarely on the desk top.

"It is a spy ship isn't it?" Finished Adam.

"Yes it is, and one that's been on a particular mission, surveying the movements that have been going on in the area you indicated. We're obliged to help uphold international law, for example, people exploiting natural resources in areas that are particularly banned under international treaty".

"About 6 months ago, we were alerted by our Ministerial colleagues that there was unusual activity taking place in the region of the North Pole, you've identified. We dispatched one of surveillance vessels to the area, to keep a watchful eye. Aside from the air-freight of supplies and building of a small settlement, there has been nothing to report and the whole exercise could be another scientific field trip to the area. Private individuals and some foreign countries are not obliged to tell us when they're planning a little field trip".

"The multiple land purchases we were unaware of, so thank you for bringing that to our attention, but I

117

think our resources are quiet safe up there at the artic circle".

The two men chatted, swapping theories and expounding upon each others long into the evening.

***

The Sailor pulled the creaky bridge door shut behind him, and cupping his frozen hands to his mouth to breath heavily on them, rubbed them enthusiastically as he turned and entered the ships wheel room.

Outside, the dark Artic days were either wet, windy or both, but always cold and the severity of the cold depended on whether you were stationed inside or out, and how strong the wind was.

He'd been outside for the last 30 minutes and it was turning into a full-blown gale outside.

A small electric heater burned on the bulkhead, barely able to bring the temperature anywhere near freezing. The window wipers were useless, freezing to the water spraying onto the small panes instantly, as ice formed and re-formed from being hastily wiped off with the back of a sleeve, on the inside.

Besides, apart from the odd iceberg, there was nothing to see anyway.

Someone thrust a steaming mug of tea into the sailors hands as they continued to shake violently from the cold. Accepting it gratefully, he took the small corridor that led from the bridge to the ward room. Here, it was noticeably warmer as oil lanterns cast an eery glow on the walls and bulkheads.

He removed his outer coat and hung it on a unoccupied hook by the door. A chef was busy staring something in a large aluminium pot, into which he reached with a large ladle and plonked a portion of something that looked like stew, onto a metal plate & handed it to the seaman.

The seaman looked at it and managed to croak "what is it?".

"Fish stew" replied the chef unsmilingly. Ungrateful lot. They had no idea how difficult it was to cook freshly prepared food for a dozen men in these conditions. When the seas were rough, the food virtually stirred itself.

The Sailor settled for returning the Chef's gruff culinary description with a sour look and headed for a table, choosing the padded bench seat that ran along the outer wall of the room, rather than one of the chairs. Last time he tried to eat in seas this rough from a chair, he'd ended up wearing most of the food.

He peered out through the small blind that covered the porthole. In the gloom and navigating lights he could just make out the storm swirling around the railings and decks of the trawler.

He'd barely raised the first forkful to his mouth when a klaxon blared and everybody jumped reaching for coats and outdoor weather gear, while the chef quickly dowsed the stove.

On the small bridge, the Captain was peering through binoculars at the waves dead-ahead. A radar operator, his face glued to a goggle shaped funnel fixed over the radar screen, was counting off the feet.

"What is it?" Asked the sailor urgently. "Unidentified object just off the Port, ahead. Could be nothing but we're definitely getting a faint echo on the radar. With all the old World War Two flotsam surfacing occasionally in these waters, it could be anything".

The sailor grabbed his own binoculars and pulling his hood into place, stepped out into the Artic evening much sooner than he would have liked. Making his way by use of the lifelines that had been strung forward and aft, he pulled himself to the bow and bracing his back against the small winch for the anchor, stood looking out to sea.

Something black, glistening, caught his attention. He refocused and stared at the spot, now hidden by a large wave. As the swell dropped he caught site of it again for an instance.

Counting the waves until the next drop, he continued to train his binoculars on where he though the currents might have taken the object whatever it was. Years of seamanship proved their worth as on the next dip in the waves, he caught site of the object again. Round, metallic, black, with protrusions radiating out from the spherical body, and instantly he knew what it was.

Hardly bothering with the safety lines, he ran back towards the bridge, shouting for all his worth. His hand was just on the bridge door when the mine touched the ships hull and the explosion consumed the small trawler, sinking it instantly.

***

Adam was driving back to home when AMIe announced an incoming priority call. Intrigued, Adam answered it and was somewhat surprised to hear the old mans voice. "You were right to warn me - we lost the trawlers signal 20 minutes ago. A drone reconnaissance has detected floating debris at the ships last known position. No reports of any survivors".

"Tek?" Questioned Adam.

"Nothing to confirm anything more suspicious than some old World War 2 ordnance at this time. I'll keep you informed if anything further comes to light".

So, thought Adam, closing the call, doubting it was coincidence or some old Mine, Tek's up to no good at the Artic. He pondered the question some more as he finally pulled onto the driveway of Jupiter House and went inside.

Chapter 10

10. The Children of WAW Strike.

It was another fine warm and sunny Saturday in Paris, as the cafes came to life and the scent of freshly baked croissants began to pervade the morning air. Already the temperature on the streets was rising as a mixture of Parisians and tourists mingled on the street's broad walkways and the smaller traffic free lanes that intersected them.

Canopies were being unfurled over freshly swept cafe exteriors as staff rushed to set tables and chairs in place.

Already, people were sat at other tables along the streets as white aproned waiters took orders and smiled politely at visitors attempts to order in French.

At the far end of the Jardin du Luxembourg, a noisy gathering of climate protestors, made up of the young & old alike, was marshalling itself ahead of a planned public march that would end at the Jordan des Tuilleris in front of the Place de la Concorde.

Some had walked others had arrived on coaches hired especially for the journey, although to the organisers dismay, many coaches had been stopped on the outskirts of Paris and prevented from making the journey to the centre.

Their protestors had formed smaller pockets of protest, waving banners and chanting at any locals that happened to pass them, determined to make their point, if only to a few goats in a neighbouring field.

The small Children of WAW group had already arrived separately and even before the cafe's started opening, had congregated and finalised their plans, picking out the two main points from which they'd launch their attacks.

A small boat waited for each on the river Seine to carry them to safety once the immediate attack was over.

Each leader of the groups had a small very pistol which would be used to fire smoke projectiles into the crowds for maximum panic, and also cover their planned escapes.

Now the time was fast approaching to get into position as the sounding of air horns announced the start of the march, and the protestors looked arms and walked in peaceful solidarity, chanting their well rehearsed slogans of protest against the lack of action on climate change.

There were more television news crews covering this march compared with the London one, and the leader smiled as he thought of all the extra coverage their mission would get.

Already, the head of the march was crossing the first bridge over the Seine at the Pont Saint-Michel.

As the tail end of the march reached the same point, so the head was beginning to cross the opposite bridge - Pont au Change - over the Seine, when the attack came.

Firing their smoke grenades into the crowds, which started shrieking and running blindly, the small terror cell detonated their charges, whilst similar charges detonated and caught the stragglers still crossing the Pont Saint-Michel, some having stopped to take in the view of the Notre Dame to the right.

Some were caught in the blasts, which hurled both them and masonry into the river below, whilst the lucky ones were only shell-shocked, their hearing impaired by the sound of the blast, walking dazed and confused and covered in a fine patina of dust, like the flour from a patisserie.

Emergency services, hampered by the loss of both bridges, were renegotiating their way to the twin scenes as local people rushed into the street to help those injured.

TV crews fortunate enough to be on the small island in the middle of the river, hurriedly set up live broadcasts, and bought the pictures of the damage and injured to the world.

As the two boats sped away carrying the terrorists to safety, the leader pickup a mobile phone and spoke quietly into it. "Mission successful. We're returning to the UK by tomorrow".

Winston Tek closed the call and leaned back in the large padded office chair, placing his hands behind the back of his head as he whirled the seat around to watch the live reporting on the TV screen behind him.

From a small office in London, a communique was sent to the national newspapers, the Children of WAW claiming responsibility for the carnage in Paris and promising similar action in the next planned climate march in Rome, the following week, unless their demands were taken seriously, and World leaders took immediate and drastic action to curb rising temperatures across the globe.

Price: Polestarr

Adam and Wednesday had watched the events in Paris unfold on the television reports, along with everyone else. The actions of the Children of WAW had taken everyone by surprise it seemed, including the protest organisers themselves, who following their arrests by a zealous Paris police force, had claimed all innocence with no knowledge of the attack or those responsible.

"However", one protest leader had declared, "We distance ourselves from the actions of the Children of WAW. They are not acting for all of us, and we the majority, remain committed to achieving action on climate change through peaceful protest only".

Interesting thought Adam that already, they were eager to distance themselves from this more violent faction within. Not that unexpected given the loss of life and injuries sustained by what might be referred to as their own kind.

"Heather is at the door" announced AMIe as Adam rose to open it, so Heather was already walking in, carrying a large shoulder bag, that looked full of files and papers.

"I'm glad I caught you at home" she said breathlessly, setting the bag down on the small table between the sofas. "I've found some material that I think you might find interesting".

"Sit down Heather won't you?" Replied Adam, taking a seat opposite the bag she'd bought with her, as Wednesday moved up to make room for her.

"No Mate?" Asked Heather looking around earnestly.

"No, he's between cohesive states. Now what have you bought me?"

"As you know, the security forces were on alert following the trouble at the London march, although they'd never suspected explosives would be involved, they were ready for similar trouble to that which occurred in London last weekend".

"I'd read they stopped many of the protestors from actually reaching Paris itself" replied Adam.

"Yes" said Heather "and that's not all".

"Security services have been monitoring any messages or calls from the area, even scrambled ones, and whilst much of the traffic was just people assuring relatives and friends they were safe, there was another message that caught my eye, because of the number it went too."

"And that was?" Asked Adam.

"I had to be sure so I ran some additional checks, but one of the calls out of the area, was to Tek Corps London offices. We're pretty sure it was re-routed securely, but where we don't know. I though you might be able to help with that".

"Tek Corp" mused Adam. "What's his involvement in all of this?"

"C'mon, lets get down to the workshop and see if we can't discover anything more".

They quickly descended the secret lift to Adam's workshops and laboratories below, passing the main garage as they did, Heather could see several robots working on the car. "More modifications?" She asked, raising an eyebrow as she spoke.

"Just a little weather enhancement" replied Adam, as they sat before the largest computer screen and Adam began patching into the intelligence source of the call log.

"With luck, we might be able to hear what was said". Adam's fingers flew across the keyboard, as with AMIe's help, he quickly hacked into the French's security service systems and located the file on the specific call they were interested in.

On an overhead screen, an outlined map of the World glowed as a red pin-prick of light appeared in

129

France, automatically zooming in, the location the call was made from appeared on an area on the banks of the Seine river, upstream from the Paris city centre.

A small red pencil line then traced outwards towards London, where it terminated at the offices of the Tek Corp.

The PC's hard drive whirred as the monitor seemed to pause momentarily, before a new pencil line began tracing outwards from London, crossing to Vandenberg before heading across state to Maine. Now it paused again before resuming North Eastwards to Iceland and finally north towards the Artic region.

The exact location, when the map zoomed in was the same site of all the ground activity, from the previous surveillance, shared by the Old Gent.

"Is that where Tek is?" Asked Heather, staring at the larger monitor hanging from the ceiling in front of them.

"Looks like it" replied Adam. "Fancy a little trip up North?".

"I though you'd never ask" replied Heather.

"C'mon, we need to get into some artic gear if we going that far north and it will give AMIe time to

130

finish the car's upgrades" said Adam, as he led heather towards a set of lockers and changing rooms.

Minutes later and they both appeared 'suited and booted', in layers of expensive artic clothing, finished off with sturdy snow boots. Wednesday commented that they looked like a pair of polar bears.

Adam gathered some telescopic walking poles from the corner of the area and pocketing mittens, over-mittens, goggles, balaclava and neck scarf, climbed into the waiting i8.

Heather did the same, and waiving goodbye to Wednesday, she took her seat and Adam closed the cars doors. Only then did she ask Adam what he intended to do?

"I need a quick look at this area and judge for myself what's going on up there. That the call from we presume someone connected with the violence in Paris, ended in the same area suggests that there's more than a few scientific Nissan huts scattered about the place".

"Plus, Mate just had time to fill me in on a presentation he stumbled upon whist snooping around Tek's offices. It seems there's plans for some sort of structure, built into the side of an ice mountain, in the Arctic".

131

"Ready?"

"Ready" she replied, as Adam drove the car up the exit ramp and out into the early evening skies above Cambridgeshire, heading northward.

They hadn't been in the air long, before a faint cracking could be heard coming from the space behind the two front seats. Heather turned to see one of Mate's suits beginning too expand as Mate slowly returned from his period of rest between materialisations.

"So where are we off to?" He asked in his usual chirpy manner. With the i8 on automatic, Adam turned round to answer his friend.

"Heather found some information amongst the messages and call logs immediately following the Paris attacks. I was able to trace one particular call of interest to an area of the Artic, where we know Tek has been operating some sort of scientific base camp. We're on our way there now to take a closer look".

"Will the cold affect you?" Asked Heather of Mate.

"I honestly don't know. We've never finished our experiments into extremes of temperature & pressure and what I'm capable of enduring".

"Well we're soon going to find out" said Adam as the car had already began its descent and a large expanse of white surface filled the windscreen as the i8 headed for the Artic and the site of Tek's land disturbance.

They flew on at low level, skipping over ice ridges and small mountains of sheer ice, forced up where ice-shelves had crashed against each other, in the ever moving 'landmass' of the region.

It was unstable and unpredictable and no charts, however accurate, had remained so for more than a week, before the land masses had moved, or disappeared. Wildlife avoided the area, nicknamed the Artic Grotto by explorers and travellers, who came to this place at the top of the World,

Now they were slowing as the homing signal on the cars navigation panel showed them approaching the site of the where the call was traced to. A small blizzard was springing up - good thought Adam, it would hide their approach and allow them to land much closer to the settlement of artic shelters.

Setting down proved trickier than first thought though as those same blizzard winds also spun the i8, trying to set down vertically, like a kite in a hurricane. At one point they were nearly blown into a nearby wall of ice, that could have caused catastrophic damage to the car and stranded them all on the ice.

Finally however using cover from the gusts provided by the same wall of ice, they were able to set down in its lee. Taking a moment to carefully make sure every part of their skin was protected with coverings and goggles, only then did Adam open Heather's door and all three climbed out onto the slippery surface.

Closing the car door behind them quickly, Adam consulted a small electronic screen hung around his neck, for directions and pointing with an out-stretched arm (for talking had become impossible in the now howling gale) the three set off, with Adam at the lead, followed on a secure tether by Heather.

Mate floated besides Heather, and the three's high visibility clothing made a stark contrast to the surrounding whites and greys of this almost unearthly landscape.

Already, the outline of one of the Nissan huts was coming into view, as Adam carefully led the way towards the door, snow piled up against its door, and using both arms, pulled the stiff doorway open, through which they all passed.

Price: Polestarr

Once inside, the removal of the howling wind and ice particles blowing was as sudden and shocking as getting out of the car had been.

A small lamp burned in the centre, and automatic sensors, detecting movement, switched on powerful space heaters, as more lights glowed on.

Save for a few desks, the room was bare. Filing cabinets stood empty and there were no papers or office equipment on any of the desks.

A coat rack stood to one side of the door, with spare outdoor jackets and boots waiting patiently to be used. On the wall of the hut, was a large architectural blueprint of some structure or other. The most notable feature was the natural rock that seemed to form the back to the 3-floored structure, that according to the foundations, also stretched far underground,

Adam took a quick picture of the blueprint, but left the original on the wall.

"Nice place" observed Mate, who up till now had been quiet. Even on the arduous trek from the car to the first hut. "I wonder I haven't seen it on Air BnB for rent".

Heather smiled, pulling down her balaclava and removing goggles that were rapidly steaming up in the

135

rising temperatures inside the hut, thanks to the massive heaters placed at every corner.

"I don't think there's much danger of getting a tan here" she replied to Mate. "What do you make of it Adam?".

"I think it's just a temporary structure for workers, possibly set to return when the Summer returns to the region, and flights are possible again. Let's check out the other huts".

They donned their protective layers once more and after a final sweep of the hut with his eyes, Adam pulled his goggles securely in place and led the three of them back out onto the ice field.

In the short time they'd been exploring the hut, the storm had lessened substantially and they could now make out the dim shapes of the surrounding huts in a circular formation. "Why not have them closer together?" Asked Heather over the noise of the storm.

"It's a fire precaution. If one hut catches fire, it shouldn't spread to the other huts in the wind".

The remaining huts held little more than the first one they'd investigated, except for one which was lined with bunk beds and another that had a large kitchen, but that too was devoid of any signs of having been in use, with no food in any of the cupboards or storage rooms.

As they neared the last hut, through the storm, a large mountain came into view. There was something odd about the shape of it and it took Adam a moment to realise that the face of the mountain facing them, was too neat and angular to have formed naturally.

He tapped Heather and Mate on the shoulder and pointed towards the distant view. "Does that mountain look odd to you?". Heather could hardly see it, her goggles so iced up but Mate, without the need for such protection replied in the affirmative.

"Want me to take a closer look?" he asked.

Adam was just about to reply yes, when the ground started shaking violently causing Adam and Heather to lose their balance and fall to the ground. In the next instant, a large crack appeared running across the small plateau they were on, and as Adam stood up, so Heather was swallowed by the widening crack as a large crevasse appeared, and she tumbled inwards.

Not secured by the rope that had previously tied them together, she fell some twenty feet, coming to rest on a small ledge inside the steadily forming ice cave. Without thinking, Adam drove his ice-axe into the ground and tying one end of the rope around it securely, began descending down to Heather's position.

Mate was already there, asking her is she was OK?

"I'm fine" she stammered as Adam got level with her. "Just a little winded".

"Do you think you can climb back up with our help?" asked Adam, eyeing the walls of the cavern which had stopped moving outwards and were now beginning to close back together.

"I can try" she replied bravely and went to stand up, only to collapse with a scream of pain, as her left ankle gave way the moment she put weight on it. Adam pulled the socks down to expose the ankle and saw a large purple bruise forming in a puffy ball.

"Heather my dear, you've broken your ankle. Now I'm going to need you to be very brave as Mate and I pull you out of this cave, before it closes completely".

She nodded, trembling as Adam untied the rope from around himself and tying an old Fireman's Lift knot, made two large loops that would fit under her arms and knees like a harness,

Leaving Mate with her, he began a hand over hand climb of the rope, still fastened to the ice-axe in the surface, and quickly reached the top, for there wasn't a moment to lose. The ice-walls had grown considerably closer even in the short time he'd tied and prepared the make-shift harness for Heather.

Now Mate floated up and joined Adam on the surface as they both took hold of the rope and began pulling Heather to safety.

She was about 10 feet from the surface when she called out. Her bad ankle had become hooked on a jagged piece of ice, and she was stuck.

Adam tied off the spare rope they'd already pulled Heather up on and rushed to lean over the gap into the cave below. She was still & outstretched, her left foot being pulled almost to a tip-toe by the force of the rope lifting her. Adam immediately released a half foot of the rope and made it fast again.

Looking over the edge carefully once more, she looked up at him and smiled, mouthing a 'Thank you' for taking the pulling strain off of the trapped foot.

The cave walls gave another mighty heave and closed more quickly, leaving very little room for Heather. Another large movement like that would trap and entomb her forever.

Mate didn't hesitate, but instantly floated down to where Heather was and started to dissipate out of his suit.

"What are you doing?" cried Adam.

"Saving Heather" replied the communicator voice of Mate, as the suit finally went flat, and fluttered down into the depths of the dark icy cavern.

Now Heather was aware of a strange tingling sensation, like pins and needles, all over her body as the ice around her began to start bulging apart in a rough spherical shape. The walls of ice trembled as though some mighty force was pushing against them, and finally, Heather's foot came free, and Adam, realising what Mate was doing, rushed back to where the rope was tied-off and began pulling Heather up for all his worth.

As her hands neared the surface, so she grappled with gloved hands to grab hold of anything she could use to pull herself free. Already the ice walls were winning the battle against Mate's intervention, and were closing in once more.

Adam leapt for the closing gap and grabbed her hand, summoning all his remaining strength to pull her the last few feet and out onto the snowy surface.

Not a moment too soon, for even as he rolled back in exhaustion, so the gap closed with a final shudder, trapping Mate underground for good.

A snowy ice-field is no place to hang around, and Adam quickly lifted Heather's doll-like form, for she had passed out with the pain of the last few terrifying moments, and carried her back towards the waiting car.

Once inside the warmth of the car's interior, Adam quickly took off her outer hat, goggles and mittens, loosening the heavy, ice-encrusted artic coat she'd been wearing. Rolling up her sleeve, he gave her a pain killing injection, before starting the car and taking flight, back home.

From a window in the mountain with its strange angular face, a technician watched the car rise and fly away, before returning to his desk and picking up the phone.

Jonathan C. Crouch

Chapter 11

11. Trapped in the ice.

Heather had stirred only briefly during the flight home, in a slightly delirious babble, induced by the pain-killers Adam had administered.

The Sun was setting as they neared that quiet corner of Cambridgeshire, and as AMIe located a suitable quiet stretch of road, so Adam bought the car back from flight mode with a barely perceptible bump and he turned off the back country lane up the farm track that led to the original hidden barn entrance to his laboratory.

AMIe had already activated the ramp, hidden in the barn's floor, as Adam swept down it and into the garage below.

Wednesday was already there, waiting with a compact stretcher, onto which they carried Heather and placed her gently, before wheeling her down to one of the underground guest rooms - the one she'd first stayed in when she'd been driven by Mate after their pub 'date', to meet Adam in person.

Wednesday finished undressing Heather and got her into a comfortable gown. With the constraints of the winter boot and socks removed, the bruising had swelled considerably, but an x-ray showed the break to be clean, and with all the necessary equipment at hand, she was able to dress and enclose the broken ankle in a flimsy cast. Another, more stronger one could be applied once the swelling had gone down, she explained to Adam.

"And what happened to Mate"? She asked.

"I honestly don't know. It's perfectly possible he'll make his way to the surface and 'float' home. Either that or the cold will impede his ability to materialise. He could even materialise and become trapped in the ice for evermore".

"We just don't know enough about his physiology to determine what his form is capable of and what it's limitations are. We had planned to carry out more experiments in the relative safety of the training rooms here, but only got as far as testing barometric pressure at sea-depths".

"I'll stay with Heather" said Wednesday rising from the lab stools she'd been on. "You'd better get to work on finding Mate", she said without a backward glance, as she walked out of the room.

Price: Polestarr

By the following morning, the swelling on Heather's ankle was already down and Wednesday carefully removed the temporary cast she'd applied the night before and put a new, more permanent cast in its place.

Heather was now awake and 'back in the real-world' as she'd put it, and complimented Wednesday on her medical administrations.

"Any news of Mate?" She enquired as Wednesday returned with a breakfast tray of toast & honey, coffee and fruit juice.

"None yet" replied Wednesday "but Adam's working on it. In fact, he's been working non-stop since we arrived back without even a break. Was he like this when Mate first re-appeared in the Lab, following the accident?".

"Yes he was. I remember those few frantic days as he developed the cloth, then the suit and the transmitter, that Mate uses now. If anyone can help Mate, it's Adam".

Wednesday only nodded and leaving Heather to rest, took the empty tray back towards the kitchen area, that had been Adam's living space, before going to find Adam

He was still working in the main lab, one screen running lines of computer code whilst another moved systematically over a map, divided into small squares. The computer monitor would set on a particular square of the map briefly before moving onto the next.

"Any luck?" She asked hopefully.

"None. It's as if the ground has swallowed him up, which is exactly what happened of course.

Even if he is able to make it to the surface, he can't materialise in anything smaller than a 2mtr sphere without the suit or the material its made from.

I'm searching for any measurement of energy or ground disturbance repeatedly in the area we were last, hoping that he merely de-materialised and hasn't re-emerged yet".

***

Out on the ice-plateau amongst the huts, a large Snow-Cat vehicle with its 4 tracked wheels, pulled up beside the point where the crevasse had finally closed, entombing Mate.

Three men got out, clad in heavy duty artic clothing, and started chipping at the spot with ice axes. When the were about two feet down, a fourth man stopped them and taking a small box-like device, connected to which was a long probe, began moving the probes tip around the surface the other three had dug out.

Save for a small digital pad, the device was devoid of any other buttons or controls. Suddenly the screen showed a small LED bar light up, much like a mobile phone registering the strength of phone signal.

Pointing with the end of the probe, the other three began digging again. Two more feet, and the man with the box stopped them once more and re-scanned the area, giving a thumbs up signal and pointing to the end of the trench they'd now dug out.

One of the Three now went to the back of the Snow-Cat and unclipping a storage pod reached and came back with what looked very much like a flame-thrower.

Pumping the device to prime it, he clicked a button on the arm and a bright blue flame jetted out from the cowled end of the gun.

Pointing it close to the surface of the trench they'd dug, he quickly melted the ice, as the the flame gun quickly burrowed downwards, the other two scooping the slushy, half-froze mixture it left in its wake out of the trench before it refroze.

Now the hole was quickly growing in depth as the hot jet of flame melted through the ice. Through the immediate layer of melted ice the men could see a darkness, suggesting a cave or opening just under the frozen surface.

The man put the flame-gun down and the three of them scooped the last of the mush out of the hole, going through the bottom with their shovels into some sort of chasm underneath.

Shining a torch inside, the lead man who had been in control of the wand detecting device, was surprised to see the chasm was almost spherical in shape, the ice walls had taken on a peculiar blue taint.

Now another larger vehicle approached more slowly, cautiously across the ice towards the small group of men. It was a cross between a crane and a digger, with an unusual digging bucket mechanism like that used to lift large trees and their immediate root system from the ground.

Following the lead mans arm signals, the crane inched into position and extended support pads at all four corners.

After briefly testing the weight on the ice by putting a small amount of pressure on the extended pads, the crane / digger uprighted its large round bucket and extending the 4 large shovel like claws outwards, drove them into the ice. The blades found their mark, and began closing, controlled by the powerful hydraulic system of the crane.

Once all 4 points had met underground, the crane retracted the digging bucket and a huge scoop like, bowl of ice emerged. The extraction completed, the two tracked vehicles turned on their tracks and began the slow, steady crawl back towards the ice mountain they'd come from, with their prize.

AMIe had been monitoring the ice shelf that Mate had been trapped in, whilst Adam worked on his methodical search for any signs of Mate. Now she broke into Adam's concentrated pose and said "I've detected vehicle movement on the surface of the ice, around the exact area we lost Mate. I'm pulling the surveillance footage onto the main Monitor".

Adam looked up, just as Wednesday re-entered the room and leaning on the bench beside him, asked if they'd found anything.

"AMIe might have something" replied Adam. "Vehicle movement on the ice surface, which she's got on camera. Lets take a look".

The large monitor flickered then came to life. Obviously filmed from a great distance overhead, shadowy blobs that were vehicles moved slowly before stopping at the exact point where they'd lost Mate in Heather's rescue. Smaller figures of people could be detected moving on the ice, to & from from the vehicles.

"I'll clean the images up now" stated AMIe, as hard drives whirred and the pixelation grew less and less on the screen.

After a couple of horizontal swipes, like someone with a window cleaner moving their blade across the screen, the image was distinctly clearer. The final pass presented an image that could have been filmed from 10ft away, as Adam and Wednesday watched the movements of the men on the ice, the arrival of the excavator and the lifting and taking away of the spherical block of ice.

"They've not only found Mate, they've excavated him and took him back towards the mouth of that nearby ice mountain" said Adam grimly.

"But surely he's not still in there?" Replied Wednesday.

"I don't honestly know. We never tested his form and abilities in these kinds of temperatures. He could be inert like gas, frozen particles of matter, or something else entirely knew. I'm more worried about what condition he'll be in & if even he can survive thawing out. You know how strawberries go when defrosted. Mate's unfrozen form could be the same".

"What ever the answers, we're not going to find them here. I need to get back up there now".

"AMIe, what's the condition of the i8?" "Primed and ready to leave". "I've increased the cars traction abilities on ice & snow and increased the passive interior force-field which should stop snow and ice blowing into the car when you open the doors. It should also retain the heat in the car cabin as well".

"You're a treasure" replied Adam, sprinting for the garage, as AMIe was already starting the engine and opening the gull-wing door on the drivers side.

"I'm not coming too?" Asked Wednesday.

"No, you need to stay here and look after Heather, plus continue your work on those climate models".

Kissing her lightly on the forehead, he swung into the open car door and was already driving up the exit ramp before the door had fully shut.

Jonathan C. Crouch

Chapter 12

12. In the Hall of the Mountain King.

Adam didn't waste a second in getting airborne and heading North at maximum speed, as AMIe plotted various landing points on the ice, based on the latest ice-shelf movements and the weather conditions which had quickly worsened again, this time over a 200 square mile area of the Artic. This was no localised storm like they'd encountered before.

Temperatures were dropping rapidly and the light of the short Artic day was already fading. Suggesting extreme caution to Adam, AMIe concluded her report with the last overhead satellite images she'd been able to hack into before the storm had obliterated the view from Space.

"A helicopter landed shortly after the two vehicles had returned towards the Ice Mountain, on the other side of the mountain. At least that's what it looked like, as I lost the picture before it touched down".

"Another visitor" pondered Adam out loud. "I wonder who that would have been?"

A singular beep came from the car's dashboard main screen as a sweeping radar like momentum showed a small red dot that was their intended landing site.

Landing would have involved using the cars vertical take-off & landing capabilities but with the storm, the winds were too strong.

The only possible way of landing was to approach low at a shallow angle trying to shed as much flight speed as possible, to enable a short as possible physical landing on the ice. A surface that was uneven, frozen rock with any number of out-jutting pieces that could flip the i8 in an instant and leave them marooned on the inhospitable Artic surface.

AMIe was already reducing their power as Adam took the controls and steered the car, swerving left & right to avoid ice ridges that had appeared out of nowhere, and could barely be seen amongst the flying shards of ice whipped up by the storm. More than once, he heard a scraping sound as the protected underneath of the car brushed against an immovable icy surface.

Their landing spot, close to the side of the mountain where the vehicles had headed back to, was approaching as Adam moved controls to set the car for a touchdown on the very ice-field they'd all been on previously.

There was a slight bump, the car reared up into the air, as the storms high winds caught the smooth underneath surface of the car and lifted it, before the front of the car fell back with a lurch and AMIe confirmed all 4 wheels were on the surface. Now all they'd got to do was stop before they crashed in the fast approaching wall of black rock and ice.

***

Mate became aware of a strange sensation, like that of a dripping sponge, as he slowly began to thaw from his spherical form.

A small group of 3 white-coated technicians were watching the platform the ice sphere had been deposited on carefully, as the outer ice began to thaw and drip from the surface, onto the rubber matted steel floor, lifted some 3 feet into the air on powerful hydraulic arms.

From a secure windowed gantry above, Winston Tek watched the scientists at their work and the dissolving ball of what they had described as "pure energy". The discovery had intrigued him enough to make the journey straightaway, and not a moment too soon, with the onset of the storm that raged outside.

They were inside his own secret headquarters, from where he ran most of his business. The mountain they were inside was hollowed out and included several floors, split into luxurious living accommodation, offices suites, laboratories and larger manufacturing areas, that also served as storage for all their supplies.

The bottom-most floor was level with the ice field and a large mechanical door could open to allow vehicles and personnel access directly onto the ice.

The whole complex was powered and heated by a small nuclear core that was suspended deep down in the ocean below, connected by a small umbilical shaft.

It was of Tek's own design and his engineers had spent months creating the spectacular home for his business empire. The cost of building it had been of little consequence to Tek, and he'd already recouped much of his investment with other projects including the partnerships forged for the Polestarr project.

One of the scientists monitoring the frozen sphere walked over to a small console and pressed the intercom button briefly. The speaker on the desk behind Tek, bleeped once and the man's voice could be heard. "We're picking up some anomalous readings emanating from inside the sphere. Readings of an energy we've never encountered before. Do you wish to continue?"

"Yes!" Snapped Tek back. "I want to know exactly what's in that ball of ice and why Dr Price was so interested in it. Continue with the de-frost sequence".

The wall of black rock was rushing towards the i8 and Adam struggled to keep control now it was on the ground. The special spiked treads of the tyres were useless against the rock like surface of ice.

A proximity alert was flashing on the main screen, as with one last desperate act, Adam flung the steering sharply to the left, putting the car into a 180 degree spin. At the exact moment the car was facing immediately away from the rock, he quickly ignited the flight rockets, their power quickly bringing the car to a halt, just feet away from the mountainside.

As the jolted to a stop, Adam let out a sigh of relief and flexed his clenched fingers which had almost welded themselves to the steering wheel.

AMIe was already scanning the area and had started bringing schematics of what looked like a large building, up on the cars main screen. "I'm

157

detecting a substantial structure inside the large mountain behind us. An in-depth radar probe is showing a building with several floors. The largest room is level with the ice field we're now on and I'm picking up radioactive elements deep below us. Possibly a reactor of some kind that could be powering the activity in the building".

"Any sign of Mate?" Asked Adam.

"There's a recognisable energy signature, consistent with Mate's cohesive form coming from within. I'll try to get the exact location to your watch".

Donning the last pieces of protective gear needed to venture outside the car, even for a second, Adam quickly prepared & dressed. With a last check that any bare skin was covered and slipping his goggles into place, he swung the door up quickly and virtually rolled out of the car.

Once on the ice, the intense cold was immediate. Even through all the layers he was wearing and his teeth were chattering almost straightaway. Not wasting a second more, he turned towards the wall of rock they'd so nearly crashed into, and started a slow steady walk along its base.

His goggles were of his own design and included an outlined display, provided by AMIe, to help him navigate in the blinding storm. Already she'd located a small opening - possibly a door in the wall some 40 metres from where he was.

Using the radar like 3D outlines on his goggles, he moved with purpose onwards until he came to the small opening. It was some sort of shutter, with no visible handles or means of opening it from the outside. That made perfect sense since any such door furniture would quickly freeze and become stuck.

No, the opening had to be activated from the inside somehow.

A thought occurred that someone returning from the outside must have some means of opening the door rather than waiting for it to be opened for them. In this harsh environment, any second spent outside unnecessarily invited death.

Pulling the strap on his right hand jacket pocket, he bought out a small box and placed it against the shutter.

Standing to the side of the opening, he reached out his arm and tapped the devices smooth surface twice.

Instantly, the shutter began moving upwards on well oiled tracks as a dim light shone outwards onto the ice. Not wasting a second, Adam rolled though

159

the still opening doorway, quickly removing the device he'd placed on it as he did so.

Straightaway, the shutter started descending again. So quickly that Adam just had time to pull his arm through before it became trapped between the thick steel.

Coming up into a crouched position, he took in his surroundings. He was to the side of a large structure with huge beams overhead running to supporting pillars that angled downwards into the floor. There were several overhead cranes on gantries for lifting or loading and the space smelt of diesel fuel.

Thankfully, the small doorway he'd entered through was shielded from the main room by a series of stacked oil drums, which Adam now carefully picked his way around. The room was empty and devoid of any activity. Huge electric heaters placed every so many metres were humming quietly, emitting just enough warmth to combat the intense cold of outside.

A doorway on the back wall showed a rectangle of light through its window, which landed like the beam of a torch on the dim floor. Adam crept towards it, keeping to the safety of the shadows around the outside walls. Upon reaching the door, he raised his body to take a peek through the window.

It led to a short corridor which ended in an intersection of double doors. According to AMIe's schematic, now displaying on his watch as a small 3D projection, his best way forward was to keep straight-ahead.

Removing his gloves and unzipping his outer coat, he checked the corridor was still clear and silently opened the door. He saw or heard no-one and quickly reached the second double-doors, which again, he raised himself slowly to peek through.

Again, there was no sign of anybody, but the corridor beyond was carpeted and lit with more aesthetic lighting. Heating units were more streamlined and less industrial looking and the door handles and light fittings had more design flair.

Taking a deep breath, he opened the door and stepped through. Instantly a low, soft hooting began and a small red light blinked steadily above the doors in the corridor.

He'd obviously trigged some alarm! There was not a moment to lose. Quickly he ran to the end of the corridor and with the barest glance through its window, raced through and took the first doorway he came to.

According to AMIe's schematic, the room Mate's signature was emanating from was the other side of the laboratory he was now in.

He heard footsteps running - heavy boots muffled by the carpet and the click of weapons being primed. The footsteps stopped at the doorway he'd just passed through, then quickly passed through into the corridor he'd sounded the alarm in.

Not wasting a second, Adam crossed to an observation window at the far end of the laboratory and crawling the last few feet, looked up and peered over the low sill edge.

The room below contained 3 or 4 white coated technicians working at various pieces of equipment, all pointed towards a central platform, on which stood a sphere of solid ice. The ice was obviously being melted slowly, visible by the water dripping onto the matted draining floor of the platform.

Was it possible that Mate was still alive but somehow held trapped in the ice? These were questions for later. For now, he had to think of a way of freeing Mate and getting away.

One of the technicians now moved to a small microphone and spoke into it.. "The energy level is rising the more we continue with the thawing process.

We estimate we are down to the last few centimetres of ice, before we break through into the chamber itself".

"Good, good" replied Tek. "The alarm has sounded in the West corridor and security is checking it now. Continue with the operation and report to me as soon as you break through" and with that Tek turned and strode out of the small observation room, without a backward glance.

His security chief was waiting outside for him. "We've combed the area around where the alarm was tripped but haven't found anything or anyone for that matter. The outer doors are secure and haven't been activated since the last party went out onto the ice just before the storm broke".

"I want a search of the immediate area outside" snarled Tek.

"But sir, with the storm that's not safe".

"I'm well aware of the safety issues" replied Tek. "My instructions stand. Send search parties out now!".

The officer nodded and turned towards the large hangar like room Adam had first entered. The storm had grown even fiercer and visibility was near zero.

Jonathan C. Crouch

A small group of men were already assembled, wearing matching artic gear with orange and red stripes down the arms & legs, and a small backpack of supplies and equipment.

Carrying short, automatic rifles with powerful torches attached to the sights, they roped themselves together in 3 teams of 4 men as the larger door was opened and the full force of the storm hit them head on.

In this weather, they could walk within a metre of a red double-decker bus and not see it, mused the officer and he led the men out, indicating with an out-stretched arm the direct each team was to take.

Silently, the three search parties set off.

Back in the laboratory room, the energy readings were going off the scale as the ice shrunk down to the last few millimetres. Suddenly, the now egg-shell thin crust shattered outwards and fell to the ground. Several pieces were caught in some kind of invisible eddy as they rose up into the air.

Mate was free from the ice at last!

Adam watched the ice ball explode outwards as AMIe reported the energy readings had peaked. He watched as the ice fragments danced in mid-air, caught in the draft of some invisible wind, spiralling upwards towards the roof of the room.

The lead scientist had slapped his hand down on an emergency button the minute they had detected the ice fracturing and large shutters had come down, sealing the room from the rest of the building.

Now the three scientists watched the eddy of ice particles dance about the room, following the tune of an invisible piper it seemed, before they eventually fell to the ground, showering the three cowering men with droplets of icy water.

Grabbing hand-held scanners, the three swept their immediate surroundings. There was no energy signature at all. Over and over the room they swept but to no avail, for Mate had already passed through the shutters into the next room.

Jonathan C. Crouch

Chapter 13

13. Escape from the Ice Palace.

Adam had just had time to see the sphere off ice explode before the shutters blocked off his view completely.

Moving to a desk of monitors, he'd figured out the controls and watched the rest unfold on the cameras, as the three scientists inside had swept for the energy signature that was Mate.

Now his own watch, which had a built in scanner was flashing a small neon blue light, indicating that Mate's presence was near.

Standing up, he swept the room, the watch locking onto the strongest signal, towards which Adam carefully walked. He was barely half-way across the room when a familiar blue-tinged ball began to appear in front of him.

"Mate, I'm glad to see you" began Adam, but just then footsteps could be heard outside as more security men ran down the corridor.

"AMIe has the car nearby, if we can just get to it". The blue-tinged ball bobbed up and down as if signalling its agreement. Adam went to the door and opening it the tiniest crack, looked down the corridor. A single guard had been left on duty, watching the corridor carefully.

Adam closed the door shut again, and gave the problem of how to get past the guard some thought. Suddenly, the blue ball passed through the wall and into the corridor. Adam opened the door a crack and looked. One minute, the guard was standing next to the door control, the next, he was flattened, pressed against the wall of the corridor, before being released and crumpling to the floor.

They moved out of the carpeted area towards the hangar through which Adam had first entered. As tempting as it was to explore this structure more, the armed guards meant whoever it belonged to, they took their privacy very seriously. Further exploration would have to wait. What mattered now was escaping and assessing how badly Mate had been affected by his incarceration in the ice.

The guard watching the last doorway was dispatched in similar fashion to the first by Mate, as Adam moved to the other small side door he'd entered through.

Speaking into his Watch, he spoke quietly "AMIe, we're about to leave the building and head back to you. Is it clear?"

AMIe instantly replied "There are 3 teams of 4 men searching the area now. One team passed quite close to me. I've engaged my auto-camouflage mode, which has allowed snow to build up over me and hide me completely".

"Well done" replied Adam. "Stay there and we'll make our way towards you".

However, once out into the storm, that was going to be easier said than done, for the storm had shifted direction and was now blowing head-on to Adam for the return journey. Adam had no way of knowing if Mate was still with him, ahead or had been forced back by the gale.

Pressing ahead, he caught a torch moving ahead, and quickly darted behind an outcrop of rock.

Four heavily clad figures trudged past him, roped together, sweeping their torches Adam could see attached to their rifles. The snow & ice had already turned his own artic gear a greyish white, so he blended in perfectly with his small hiding place.

The search team passed by, and giving them an extra minute to get further past, so Adam rose and

169

moved onwards, AMIe's homing signs drawing him ever closer.

The last few feet of ice-wall looked familiar as he approached a hummock of snow that hadn't been there before, he was mere feet away when the side shook and the door of the 18 opened and swung upwards.

Adam quickly jumped in, as AMIe closed the door behind him. The heaters were already on maximum and Adam quickly worked his way out of his outer jacket, and protective gear, the moisture from the snow quickly evaporated thanks to the car's air-conditioning.

The spare containment suit for Mate, Adam had brought along and which now laid on the passenger seat was still flat. "Is Mate in the car?" Asked Adam. "Negative" replied AMIe. I can detect no trace of Mate in the vicinity. My last reading was when you both left the structure and returned to the ice-field".

Suddenly, torch beams were flickering on the windows of the car. "They've found us" shouted Adam. "Quick give me take-off boosters. We have to get out of here".

"Engines aren't coming on line" replied AMIe. "The cold seems to be affecting the inter-mixer. I'm working in it now".

"Work faster" replied Adam, "we don't have long before they discover us".

As the windows of the car cleared, Adam could see that 8 men were slowly surrounding the car's position. Another minute and they'd discover the camouflage the i8 was wearing and open fire. They must escape now.

The leader of the first team reached out a hand to brush at the snowy mound before them. He had barely touched the surface when he was suddenly and violently thrown backwards, crashing against the mountainside.

The others now looked about themselves, their rifles poised and torch beams moving quickly from one dark form to another.

A second and third man now flung backwards, whilst a fourth was squashed down onto the icy surface, like an insect being caught under the bottom of a giant jam-jar.

The remaining four broke rank and untying their joining ropes, ran into the dark night as fast as they could against the force of the wind.

171

Adam witnessed this all from inside the car, as suddenly, Mate's suit started expanding, filling out before the voice collar activated and Mate said "what are you waiting for? Lets get out of here".

Adam didn't wait to be asked again, and as AMIe finally bought the rockets online, so the car took to the skies, climbing quickly to avoid the storm.

Back in the Ice Mountain, Tek was listening to the reports from the search team that had returned with the fallen men, and the reports from the scientific team that had been studying the frozen sphere of ice.

That the two were connected was obvious. Whatever had been trapped in that ice, had escaped.

But what was the connection with Dr Price?

He savoured the question, rolling it around inside his mind, as he leant back in the large padded chair behind his desk.

A slow smile finally began to spread across his face and he reached for the phone and said into it "Have my jet standing by the minute the storm clears".

Replacing the receiver, he continued to work on the problem of how to re-capture the energy source they'd discovered and how to get rid of Dr Price for the last time. It was his plans for the latter, that had caused the smile.

Only when they were clear of the ice storm and heading for home, did Adam ask Mate about his experience in the ice. Mate wasn't exactly sure how the ice had held him, and was only vaguely aware of the thawing out by the men back at the base they'd just left.

"I wasn't aware of any pressure or temperature. I sensed I couldn't move but I can't explain what was stopping me. I can pass through anything we're come across so why I couldn't pass through the ice is a real mystery".

"It's something we'll have to study in more detail to get the answers" replied Adam. "The main thing is you're free and safe and don't appear to have suffered for the experience. By the way, how did you know you could take care of those guards the way you did?"

"It seemed logical that I could expand my volume and maintain enough solidity of form to push the guards out of the way. I didn't quite expect the end result to be so violent, but at least it worked".

Adam grinned back at him, and they continued to discuss the merits of being invisible as the car cleared the artic circle and cruised homeward.

As they touched down on that familiar stretch of road so close to Adam's underground base, Mate began to lose cohesion, and the suit slowly deflated, just as Adam turned the i8 into the barn entrance and steered down the ramp that AMIe had activated.

He pulled into the garage area as Wednesday came jogging through from the living quarters area to greet him, arms outstretched.

She was about to ask if he'd been successful when she noticed Mate's suit on the passenger seat, in its crumpled, deflated form.

"What happened?" She asked. Adam reassured her that Mate was fine and that he'd only just dissipated as they'd touched down

"How's Heather?" Asked Adam.

"Not as well as I'd like. She seems feverish and the ankle is quite swollen. I think she may be reacting to the break leaking into her blood-stream. I think we ought to get her to a hospital".

"You're quite right of course" replied Adam. "Lets get her ready to move now".

They walked through to the bedroom where Heather was resting. She smiled when she saw Adam and tried to sit up in the bed to no avail. She was

174

running a slight temperature and when Adam looked at the ankle, it was definitely more swollen than before.

"We're going to get you admitted to Hospital" said Adam. "Wednesday is packing some bits for you now and I'll take you as soon as we're ready to set off".

Heather asked after Mate. "Was he alright?"

"He seems fine and none the worse for wear after his freezing ordeal". He quickly filled he in on how he'd discovered Mate's frozen sphere being melted in the laboratory and the escape when he'd finally emerged".

"We still don't know what was causing Mate to be unable to pass through the ice, and its something we'll have to study some more".

Settling Heather into the car, Adam climbed in and promising to be straight back, drove up the exit ramp and out onto the roads. There was no need to flight, with the small private hospital only 15 minutes away on the outskirts of Cambridge.

The journey was quick and Heather found herself being met by a white-coated Doctor and a Nurse at the entrance door, to the small, neat building complex, Adam having called ahead once they'd got above ground & on their way.

As the Nurse wheeled Heather inside so the Doctor turned to Adam and said "How did it happen?"

"A skiing accident" replied Adam, which was a half truth. 'We thought she was fine but the swelling started and she became feverish, which is when we decided we ought to call you".

"You did absolutely right of course" smiled the Doctor "and we'll soon have her well and back on her feet".

"Heather" shouted Adam, "we'll call you tomorrow. Take care" as he waved at her disappearing down the white corridor, before turning and walking back to the car.

Chapter 14

14. A Subtle Plan.

Tek had slipped in un-noticed, via a private flight and commute by helicopter, into his London offices, evading the various authorities wishing to interview him about the quick exit he'd made from Vandenberg, where Dr Adam Price had been found in mortal peril.

Striding into his office, with its full glass window offering a commanding view over the heart of London's business and banking areas, he quickly threw himself into the large office chair and swung around to face the wall, on which hung another oil painting depicting part of the naval battle at Trafalgar.

Clicking a button on the chair's arm, the large canvas lifted up to reveal a bank of monitors and television screens.

The largest one came to life, to reveal a small man in smart, white laboratory coat with the Tek groups logo embroidered on the chest pocket. "You've had 12 hours Dr. What do you have for me?"

"Not much" replied the Dr. "Using the data recorded at the artic station, we were able to scan for any other occurrences, We recorded just one, shortly after the incident, out on the ice-field itself.

After that nothing.

But we did find something that may interest you. Shortly after registering the phenomenon on the Ice-Field, we detected an unidentified craft leaving the area and flying South. It passed your Artic listening post, clearly on a trajectory that would take it back over Greenland.

In the brief time we were able to track it, it gave off a very similar energy pattern to the object you thawed out.

We checked our records and we've recorded that same energy pattern only once before, when one of the Polestarr satellites was hacked, and we had that particular object shot down".

"Keep working on that energy signature" growled Tek. "It's our number one priority to find the source".

***

Pulling up in front of Jupiter house, Adam sat for a moment thinking about the problems Tek posed, before climbing out of the car and heading indoors.

178

The front door opened automatically to him, as the houses security protocols, handled by AMIe, recognised him.

Wednesday was back in the house and had been curled up in one of the deep comfy sofas when Adam arrived.

Now she walked to meet him in the hallway and enquired after Heather. "Hell of a day" remarked Adam, smiling. "I could do with a drink".

"There's already a glass of wine poured for you. Why don't you tell me more about how you found Mate".

And so Adam recounted the story, starting with the perilous landing on the ice, breaking into the building hidden inside the large mountain, and how he'd found Mate, still trapped inside a frozen sphere of ice that had been carved out of the ground and carried back to the hidden laboratory.

Pausing to take a sip of the excellent red wine, he continued with their escape from the security patrols, before finally being able to take off and come home.

"The thing is" said Adam, "If it is Tek behind the base, then I'm pretty sure he'll have detected my energy signature as we left. It's the only explanation I

179

can think of for how we were first detected when we investigated that satellite up close".

"Do you really think Tek is behind the digging up of Mate?" Wednesday asked worriedly.

"I do, and what's more, I can't help but dwell on what he would have had in store for Mate once he'd defrosted him".

"I'm also concerned that Mate's shown no signs of re-materialisation yet. It's long past the usual time-span between physical visits. Perhaps the cold has affected him or being trapped for so long, unable to completely lose cohesion, has undone all the work we'd done on managing his presence".

With the wine finished and heads still full of unanswered questions, the two of them doused the lights and headed for their bedrooms. Perhaps the answers would be more apparent on the dawn of a new day.

It seemed that their heads had hardly touched the soft pillows, before the morning sunlight streamed through the blinds, low and spreading warmth wherever it crept and touched.

Wednesday awoke, showered and changed into comfortable clothing before heading to the kitchen where she met Adam, already sat at the large island,
180

drinking coffee and scooping the last spoonful of yoghurt, muesli and fruit from a bowl, whilst looking intently at the screen of an electronic tablet beside him.

Wednesday asked hm how he'd slept, followed by asking after Mate. "There's no change I'm afraid. Mate's still not returned".

"What are you going to do?" Asked Wednesday.

"I've been working on some ideas for counter-detecting any tracking or monitoring of my fusion reactors energy signature, and I was just heading to the main lab to start putting theories into practice. Care to join me?"

"I really ought to be getting back to my own labs" replied Wednesday. "Do you think its safe?"

"Surveillance hasn't picked up any suspicious persons in the area, but I'd much rather you continued here for now" replied Adam, trying to sound hopeful, rather than worried, about Wednesday returning to her own building.

"At least stay until the counter-tracking measures I mentioned are in place. Then I'll feel happier about you being on your own". She nodded her agreement to the plan, subtle as it was, it kept her at Adam's house for a few more days.

AMIe was already running simulations on the various theories Adam had worked on, the tablet linked directly into her matrix, like the larger computers throughout the house and underground in the bases laboratories.

One idea had been the laying of fake signature trails, since the frequency and composition of the fusion reactor was so unique, and so powerful as to make it invisible seemingly impossible.

Fake readings could be simultaneously triggered across the globe, so anyone tracking them would not know which was genuine and which was fake. Of course, the fake ones could be ruled out given enough time, by which the real cause of the energy signature would be long gone.

Adam took the tablet and a small external hard drive from the large PC on his workbench and headed for the garage. "No time like the present to install it and see if it really works" he shouted over his shoulder to Wednesday as he left the room.

Wednesday had been working on her own problem, namely the increase in the sea temperatures around the artic, that affected the 3 sensors she had privately paid to have deployed there.

Price: Polestarr

In her mind she heard Adam talking about the structure built into the mountain and the deep running umbilical to a reactor suspended in the icy depths, acting like a natural coolant to counteract the heat generated by the small nuclear furnace.

She swung around on her stool and asked AMIe to show a 3D image of the ocean and the coastline around location of the Artic base.

A large model began appearing on the largest viewing table, as ice ridges, which ran deep under water, became clearer as the model became more and more realistic with each layer built by the powerful computer.

She marvelled at it. The same task would have taken all the Universities computing power a week to achieve the same model and even then not in as much detail as this.

"Model complete" came AMIe's cool voice.

"Now, can you project the movement of the currents for the last 6 months, and show any temperature variations"?

"Simulating now" replied AMIe, as the visual model began moving, the currents indicated by multi-layered moving swathes of shaded neon areas.

"Adding sea temperature information now" said AMIe, and instantly the model glowed with hues of blue and red, the red indicating temperature increases.

"Now", said Wednesday, "add the relative position of my three temperature buoys over the same period and loop the animation".

Three orange points appeared on the model, swaying back & forth on the anchored tethers they were fixed to.

Adam walked back into the lab, having completed his electronic updates on the i8, just in time to see the full animation running, as Wednesday turned to him, her eyes shining with excitement.

"You realise what we're seeing here?" she asked.

"If I'm not mistaken, this is the land & sea mass around the ice-field we landed on, reaching back to the open sea and the location of your temperature buoys?"

"Exactly" she exclaimed, barely able to contain herself, her body jigging like an excited school child that's been told they can have an ice-cream in the park.

She began pointing out features on the animation - the flow of the currents, the position of key elements.

184

"You see, once all the information is factored in and a 3D model built, we can really see the interaction that's occurred, and the likely source".

"Here" she said placing her hand inside the model and pointing to a small dot. "This is the reactor, powering the hidden building on the ice-field. You'll see it's generating a small amount of heat, warming the ocean around it, like a stone left in the Sun to get warm, would heat a saucer of water if it was placed in one".

"We can see the currents at this time of year carry that heat under the ice-flows and out to sea. The rising temperatures my buoys have been recording are just the discharge from the area of this reactor. That's what's causing the anomaly".

"But you said that the figures Tek's PoleStarr satellites were transmitting back to Earth were tampered with", replied Adam, still captivated by the swirling, ebbing 3D model.

"Yes they are, but at least my data is clean & verified now".

"What do we do with this information?" Replied Adam.

"We alert the Governments" said Wednesday solemnly. "The fact that whoever is running that

185

reactor is causing a chain effect of temperature rises, is enough to force an investigation. The data tampering from the satellites is another matter. If only we could figure out why?"

The work had taken most of the day and it was time to eat before visiting Heather in the nearby hospital. As AMIe closed down the simulation, so the pair of them headed for the lift and back up to the surface.

Chapter 15

15. Visiting Hours.

After a quick dinner of chicken salad and a sparkling fruit juice made by a local orchard, Adam and Wednesday got in the i8, still parked out front of the house and headed down tree-lined narrow country lanes towards the hospital.

They were barely 5 minutes into the short journey, when a pair of headlamps appeared in Adam's rear-view mirror, doggedly mirroring their speed and progress along the dusky roads.

As he cast another glance in the mirror and realised it was now being followed by a second car, and gaining on them, the hairs on the back of his neck stood up. Something told him this wasn't some yobbish driver, but something perhaps a little more sinister.

"Buckle up" Adam said quietly to Wednesday. "I think we have company". Wednesday turned round to look out of the back window and saw the twin pairs of headlights. She secured the simple lap belt fitted to the seat, and pressed herself back into the seat as Adam began increasing speed and the i8 responded by instantly leaping forward.

Now the ruts and pot-holes became more noticeable in the cars cabin despite the advanced suspension and comfortable seats. If it was like this in their car, what must it be like in the tailing cars that had taken a moment to realise what was happening before increasing their own speed to match.

The road ahead was narrow & twisty with not enough room for a run-up to take off. Vertical flight required the car to come to a stop first. No, thought Adam, there only chance was to outrun them.

Despite the unevenness of the lane's surface, and the crumbling edges of the road, the sides falling away to deep ruts made by farm vehicles and lorries, the lead chasing car was attempting to come alongside the i8 as Adam weaved to close off any gaps. Suddenly, the black car was flung into the air, spinning crazily, before crashing into the neighbouring field and continuing its death roll, with pieces of bodywork and tyres flying off to litter the field and hedgerow.

"Must have hit one of those large pot-holes" stated Adam, but he needed to concentrate for already the second car had taken up close quarter to the rear of the i8 and was looking for its own opportunity to overtake or force Adam and Wednesday off the road.

They were now travelling at speeds of over 90mph, bumping and catching brief moments of air between the wheels and the road surface, like some rally car stage. Still the road afforded no opportunity to go to flight mode and the only assistance to Adam was the navigational projection on the cars windscreen showing the graduations of the road, verges and corners as they approached. The advantage was just enough to keep them in front.

Suddenly, from around the next corner, appeared a tractor and trailer, hauling large bales of straw. Adam fought with the controls to slew the heavy car sideways and glide around the obstacle, while the chasing driver did the same.

Too late! A second tractor unit was pulling out of a concealed field entrance with its own heavy trailer load of straw bales. Straddling the narrow little lane to complete its turn out onto the road, it was completely across the road, blocking any possibility of passing.

There was no time to think. Pure reaction took over and his faith in the car's abilities as Adam ignited the take-off rocket, which in the last few seconds before impact, lifted the car into the air, bursting through the uppermost layer of straw, spectacularly

189

coming out of the other side in a storm of flying pieces of straw.

The pursuing car didn't stand a chance of stopping in time and smashed into the trailer, igniting in an explosive golden ball of fire, as the i8 completed its leap through the air and came to land on the far side, with a jarring crash, that despite the lap belts and passive restraint system fitted into the car, threw Adam and Wednesday about the cockpit.

Adam bought the car to a sliding, sideways stop and wound down the windows. The miniature haystack on the trailer was blazing, sending plumes of black smoke billowing into the evening air as the straw crackled and quickly reduced to a fine grey ash around the metallic carcass of the trailer, still attached to the green tractor unit that had been pulling it, and bought a dramatic, fiery end to the chase.

Closing the window, Adam turned the car towards the open road and drove off at a more leisurely pace. Wednesday, sufficiently recovered from the chase's finale, was the first to speak. "Who were they?".

"I don't know" replied Adam, "but I'd put money on it being something to do with Tek".

Price: Polestarr

They'd barely driven two miles when, from a small intersecting junction, another car pulled out after they'd passed, and began closing on them.

Adam merely grunted and motioned to Wednesday to look behind them. Still the twisty country lane with its tight, high banks, offered no opportunity of escape by converting to flight mode, as the large black saloon quickly caught up with them, it's front weaving and dipping, putting pressure on the cars suspension, under the aerodynamic forces of the speed.

A sudden burst of gun fire sounded as bullets whistled past Wednesday's side of the car. A man was leaning out of the passenger window of the car behind, with some sort of short stubby automatic rifle. As he took aim again so Adam braked hard and slewed right, putting the gunman off his target and causing the car to brake violently.

Adam took the advantage and put distance between them, but already the assailants were catching up, firing as they came. Bullets struck the rear window, bouncing off the bullet-proof glass harmlessly, but the rear panels of the car were beginning to take a battering from the hail of bullets.

AMIe reported that the flight engine had been disabled by the constant firing, that only paused when presumably, the gun's magazine had run out of bullets and was being reloaded.

The road was beginning to widen, which would make it much easier for the car to overtake them, and with no flight options.. Adam looked about him, trying to find anything that might help them escape. These brutes meant business and had either exceeded their orders and were resorting to firepower or had been ordered to stop Adam at any cost.

Suddenly they passed a sign for a go-karting centre, and almost immediately, Adam spun the steering and took the i8 into a sideways drift & up the track to the centre.

It was an outdoor track with twisty turns, and straight stretches. In the middle of the course, the enterprising owners of the business had constructed a rugged off-road course, with ditches, moats and steep gradients that bent around strategically placed piles of rough sawn logs or large conifers.

Adam took the track option as the smooth tarmac surface meant he could increase speed, the i8's advanced suspension and road holding coming into its own.

The chasing car had followed them onto the circuit but any hopes of cutting across the grass centre of the track, to cut off Adam & Wednesday were derailed by the wall of old tyres that lined either side of the track, 2 or 3 layers thick.

Around the next hairpin bend and they came across a trio of go-karts weaving about the track, jockeying for the best racing line. The racing suited drivers, in full face helmets and tinted visors completely unaware of the chase behind that was catching them up fast.

Now Adam was level with the trailing kart as the driver, overwhelmed with surprise at seeing the large BMW car beside him, bobbed and weaved, leaving the track and burying himself in the pile of safety tyres.

"One down, two to go" smiled Adam as he gripped the steering wheel and chased down the second kart. Behind them, the assailants were closing, taking advantage of the i8's slowing down when it had encountered the go-karts.

The leading kart had misjudged the last bend and gone wide, allowing an inside pass barely possible, but the nimbleness and size of these powerful little vehicles, meant the second kart was able to zip through the gap, closely followed by Adam.

The now second place driver took it as a personal a-front that the road car had also overtaken him, and pressing his kart to the very limits of road-holding & speed, rounded the i8 on the outside of the bend, to overtake.

"I think he wants to race us" said Wednesday, as Adam fought with the over-steer, to keep the i8 on the track. Ahead, the pit lane and exit were coming up on the home straight, as Adam floored the i8 and shot past both karts, while a marshall at the side of the track waved a chequered flag enthusiastically.

The chasing car had also followed suit with a burst of speed but lacked the i8's suspension and road-holding capabilities, as Adam and Wednesday turned and drove calmly out of the track complex, so the last of their pursuers, slid sideways uncontrollably before coming to rest in its roof amidst a pile of tyres and straw bales.

Chapter 16

16. Mineral Rights.

The whole escape from the would-be assailants had hardly taken any time up at all, and Adam and Wednesday pulled into the hospital car park in good time.

Securing the i8, which gleamed under the overhead lights of the multi-storey car park, Adam gave the bonnet an affectionate pat, before they moved off towards the pedestrian exits that led to the hospital wards.

They were walking through the main concourse, filled with a few shops that sold flowers or gifts, a newsagents and even a hair stylists, with a few well known high-street coffee shop chains, having their own cafes and even a fast-food outlet to cater for visitors, or patients unable to survive on hospital rations alone.

Heather's voice rang out, hailing them, from the corner of one of the quieter coffee shops. Waving as they approached, they were relieved to see her sat in a wheel chair, her plastered ankle out-stretched on a support built into the wheel chairs frame. A large cup of coffee sat steaming on the small round table beside her, as Wednesday took a seat and Adam queued to buy drinks.

Returning to the small table, he found Wednesday had already told Heather about the chase that had just ensued on their way to visit her. When she finished with them winning the chequered flag, Heather burst out laughing, their noisy jollity a stark contrast to the others.

As the laughter subsided, so Heather fought to get her words out "so it was Tek?" More of a statement than a question.

"Yes" replied Adam, "and he's certainly getting more intent on catching up with me or Wednesday or both".

"What are we going to do?" Asked Wednesday. She for one had had enough of being chased around every time she left the safety of Adam's house and laboratory. A normal life seemed a world away.

Heather noticed her friends complexion turn grey and interjected with a lighter tone "Adam will think of something. He always does" the last spoke looking earnestly at Adam.

Price: Polestarr

Adam took the hint and taking Wednesday's hand said "Don't worry about Tek. I can take care of him. What we've got to figure out is what he's really up to".

"I had some thoughts on that" replied Heather, "and I put a call into an old colleague at one of the national newspapers. His reply was quite insightful".

"It seems that several corporations have been renegotiating mineral rights at the Poles, using the Polestarr data to back up their claims that the benefits to mankind in mining the area, previously banned due to climate change, outweigh any potential ecological damage, that there is now no proof of actually occurring".

"They've made a strong case and it looks like a decision to allow restricted mining is close to being made".

"They'll endanger the World and destroy valuable habitats and natural resources" Wednesday exclaimed in horror. "Adam, we can't let this happen. You must present our data to the governments that control the mining rights in those areas. Stall the corporations".

Their coffees barely gone untouched, visiting hours were over and it was time to escort Heather back to her ward for the night. As they said farewell at the ward entrance, Adam said that he'd devote all his resources to the problem at hand, and if her contact got in touch with any more information, to pass it on immediately.

With promises to return again tomorrow, Wednesday and Adam left to return to Jupiter House.

They were driving back, this time at a more leisurely pace when AMIe announced a call coming in from Heather. Switching it to the loudspeaker Adam and Wednesday both said "Hi" before Heather spoke. "My friend came back with a list of 5 corporations that have filed for the mining ban to be lifted. One of them rang a bell, and he dug around a little more with my guidance. It seems two of the five are actually fictitious holdings owned by the Tek Corporation".

"And" replied Adam, "I'll bet the other three are as well. This whole thing is being orchestrated by Tek. Thanks Heather and keep digging".

"It makes sense" continued Adam to Wednesday, "with a substantial mining operation already in place, moth-balled inside the mountain building I rescued Mate from, the minute the restrictions are lifted, he can go into mining production straightaway. Workers could be quickly flown in and the infrastructure of accommodation and power is already there".

"You've got to admit, it's pretty clever".

"And the Polestarr data provides the necessary nudge to the Governments, to give the green-light to the mining re-starting" finished Wednesday.

"But there's one thing I don't quite understand yet" she continued. "The satellites - the expense is so enormous that a thousand years of drilling for oil won't recoup that".

"No" replied Adam grimly, "and that's what really bothers me. Whatever Tek is up to is more than just mining and oil exploration rights".

Pondering this last elusive piece of a complex puzzle, they arrived at Adam's house and quickly retired for the evening, still pondering the same question. What was Tek really up to?.

Jonathan C. Crouch

Chapter 17

17. Intermission.

When asked to envisage the launching of a nuclear missile, the man in the street would probably have notions of presidential orders, briefcases hand-cuffed to uniformed guards and the simultaneous key turning and large red button pressing to launch a barrage of destruction, from the safety of military bunkers, buried deep underground.

It would surprise (and worry) many to discover that the actual process is more automated and computer aided, with only corresponding sets of key-codes being required to authorise an actual launch.

The failsafes are that two sets of codes required have a secondary requirement that they come from the area the President or Military leader is known to be in and the codes are changed every 24 hours. An encrypted line is always held open as a direct connection to a small portable device the leaders aide carries that provides that days set of codes.

For the NATO alliance, the signals pass through Cheltenham GCHG. The Chinese and Soviets having their own versions of the same system.

With most of the nuclear arsenal now being submarine rather than land based, the belief that the system is infallible is backed-up by routine tests, whilst the computers that house & generate the codes are redundant from any external internet connection, and effectively cut-off from any outside hacking attempts by the greatest firewall of all - namely not being connected to the network in the first place.

The staff that man these centres are almost blasé about the security of the system and repeatedly state that no weapon could ever be launched inadvertently or by some terrorist organisation.

At 23, Airman Scott Roberts was one of the youngest in the computer monitoring centre. He was extremely bright and this had given him a certain over-confidence in his abilities. A trait welcomed by the forces and the bases commander in particular, which had no doubt helped him rise to the dizzying position he now found himself in.

An indicator light flashed on the console before him, and he casually leaned forward, closer to the screen in front of him, performed a few key strokes of the terminals keyboard and the intermittent flashing stopped. He leaned back in his chair and looked at the clock on the main wall of monitors ahead of him. 4 hours in and it was the most exciting thing to have occurred, if you didn't count bumping into Cathy at the coffee station earlier.

He was broken by his romantic reverie of Cathy, when the indicator light re-lit and flashed steadily.

Frowning he leant forward and pressed a button on his headset. "Could the controller come to station 15 please".

He ended the call and started typing queries on the terminal. The controller approached and leaning over the young airman's shoulder said "what seems to be the problem?"

"I got a system anomaly reading a few minutes ago, which I checked and cancelled and now its back again." "What's the source?" Queried the controller, taking over the keyboard and punching some lines of code into the system. "Unknown Sir. If I didn't know better I'd blame it on a static build up on my console or a faulty indicator light. There's absolutely no trace of any malfunction or integrity dropout".

"Get a maintenance crew to check out your console and move to station 16". Confident that the matter was closed, the Controller moved away whilst

Airman Roberts collected his things and moved desks as instructed. As he did, he noticed that the indicator had stopped flashing.

Price: Polestarr

Intermission ends.

Jonathan C. Crouch

Chapter 18

18. Testing Times.

The row of technicians, monitoring the Polestarr satellites from Tek's polar base, went about their work with quiet efficiency. The system was working flawlessly and just as predicted. The gargantuan effort of launching and linking 15 satellites, to feedback data to Earth simultaneously, had been accomplished. Now the really hard work of analysing the data and making it available to the scientific community around the World, was underway, as already, Governments were able to us the data to back up their political claims that each's climate policies were working.

There was almost a casualness about them as they moved un-hurried between work stations and consoles, conferred with each other some piece of data or other, and the quiet hum of the computer cooling fans and the large room air-conditioning units was only occasionally broken by the sound of someone speaking.

The room was broken down into a 'station' of 3 technicians, with each station responsible for one of the 15 satellites. They sat in inwardly curved clusters, 5 stations to a row. The fourth row was elevated, to give the supervisors (1 for each row), a better view of operations & who could oversee multiple satellite operations at once, with a 3rd row even more elevated behind them, reserved for the operation manager and flight director of the shift.

Behind them was a darkened glass facade set an an angle so as to look slightly down on all of them. The glass was impenetrable - impossible to see through from the operations room side, and therefore one never knew if one was being watched or not.

It was rumoured that Winston Tek often sat behind the glass, but they were all to scared to ask outright if the great man was present or not. So they sat at their stations, worked diligently and never complained about anything.

A nasty rumour amongst the more junior staff was that someone had been caught in an area off-limits and as punishment, were banished to the surface, to freeze to death or die trying to reach one of the remote rescue shelters.

Suddenly, the routine of the day was broken by a series of amber alarms appearing on the large monitor screen, flashing error codes and data.

Price: Polestarr

Stations one to three jumped to their consoles as 3 satellites suddenly appeared to go rogue and fire positional thrusters to re-align themselves.

Controllers scrabbled to get confirmation and find out if the problem was real or just a glitch in the software, whilst others concerned with telemetry started calculating the precise points the satellites would re-position to and the fuel / thrust capabilities required to correct once they stopped moving. If they stopped moving.

Suddenly the flight controller was shouting for their attention, calling them to order. As they all turned around, away from their monitors, a large section of the darkened glass rose upwards, to reveal a largish man, impeccably dressed. It was the man himself - Winston Tek.

He stepped through the doorway smiling and shaking hands with the director, before addressing the room before him. From the raised dais he looked like a Roman Emperor addressing his people.

"My friends" he began, "My apologies for the inconvenience but the failure is in fact nothing more than a carefully executed drill, to demonstrate to our investors how carefully monitored our system is and how quickly we can respond to problems and correct them".

He was carrying a large cane which he now tapped on the floor 3 times, like some magician. Instantly, the alarms stopped and the monitors returned to their normal displays, showing the 15 satellites in perfect formation far above the Earth.

"Please return to your duties and thank you for your participation". With that, Tek leant forward and whispered a few words in the flight directors ear before taking his hand and shaking it enthusiastically.

Turning only to raise a hand towards the rest of the room, he disappeared through the doorway in the glass wall, upon which it closed again.

Once out of view, Tek turned to the other men in the room and spoke quietly. "I hope my little demonstration has proved the operational capabilities of my satellites and controlling team here? You may go back to your governments with a favourable report, no?".

With that dismissal, the men turned and left via a long tunnel like corridor. At the end, each donned protective overcoats, trousers and boots, as the snow sledge pulled a windowed container up and the men climbed in, before being whisked away to a waiting transport plane, that would fly them back to civilisation.

Price: Polestarr

Despite their intense dislike for the billionaire, and the fact that he was wanted by the British law enforcement agencies, he had delivered on all of his promises regarding the abilities of the Polestarr project.

Once they were on the plane and it had taken off, stewards served drinks, and after a few warming shots of whiskey, Tek didn't seem like a such a bad person to be dealing with after all.

***

The view of the sunrise was breathtaking as slowly, the dark skies gave way to light, slowly at first, seeping through the trees and hedges before casting shortening shadows over the fields, lighting up the fields, their crops waving and moving like an ocean, in the morning breeze.

Adam surveyed all of this from the large windows of his home, but hardly took it in, having spent the entire night working on the problem of what Tek was really unto. As Wednesday had pointed out, the costs of developing and launching one satellite, let alone fifteen would take hundreds of years to recoup just in mining.

No, something did not add up.

He was train of thought was broken by the fountain lift activating and Mate walking into the room. "Hell of a view" he said to Adam.

"It's good to se you back at last" nodded Adam.

"How long was I out?"

"It's been nearly two days my friend. Two days during which a lot has happened" and he launched into a recap of their escape from the unknown assailants that were after them ending with an update on Heather's condition. "We're going to visitor later, why don't you come too?"

"Perhaps another time" replied Mate. "I'm not sure a hospital is the best place to appear dressed like this, or disappear for that matter".

"Perhaps not" replied Adam, "That would take a bit of explaining".

Wednesday appeared at the doorway, already dressed in lab coat and jeans. "Hi Mate" she waved towards him, "it's good to see you back with us". He thanked her and asked how she was coping with the excitement of the past few days. "Not as bravely as I'd hoped" she replied a little sheepishly, "but Adam assures me you'll both protect me so I really have nothing to worry about".

212

Price: Polestarr

"Any progress on the Tek conundrum?" She asked Adam, as she reached for the coffee pot.

"I think I have" smiled Adam. "I kept asking myself what would justify the expense of the Polestarr satellite system, assuming its not just for reasons of vanity or esteem and I came across a rather disturbing conclusion. What if the Polestarr project was intended for something else other than monitoring climate change?"

***

The day also dawned bright and sunny in Vienna, where a large gathering of world ministers and scientists was going to gather for a 3 day summit on helping developing countries tackle climate change change.

Security was tight following the events of the previous weekend in Paris and both the Police and Army were out in force, armed with weapons drawn in a show of strength to deter anyone from causing trouble.

There were thousands of protestors expected and many had already started gathering at designated parks outside the ancient city. The plan was to stop them entering the very heart of the city and getting near to the state rooms of the 18th century Belvedere Palace, home to the negotiations.

A small knot of protestors had congregated outside the railway station, and having had shoulder bags searched by security personnel at the station turnstiles, when the final member of the team joined them, they turned and walked away from the rest of the crowd, towards a block of apartments.

Letting themselves in with a key, after satisfying themselves that no-one was watching or following them, they all climbed the stairs to the fourth floor, and entered the apartment that faced onto the street.

As the last person closed and locked the door, so the leader was already reaching under the bed. Pulling an old trunk, the sort that might have been used on old voyages, he snapped open the catches and lifted the lid.

Inside was an array of automatic guns and pistols with ammunition and holsters. Underneath this were metal tins marked 'high explosive'. Timers and detonators lay to the side in a separate tray compartment.

"You all know what to do" growled the lead man, who'd reached under the bed to recover the trunk. "We'll split into two teams as agreed, and take separate trams to the Ferris Wheel. After our mission is complete, make your way to the boats waiting on the Danube, which runs behind the park.

The munitions and arms were divided amongst the two teams of four, and after a last look around the apartment to make sure they hadn't left anything, the eight men & women descended the stairs and went back out onto the street.

As the trams rattled along the streets, they peered through the windows for a first glimpse of their destination, the antique Viennese Ferris Wheel, with its large suspended cars, that gave an unparalleled view of the beautiful city around them. Not for much longer smiled one of the terrorists to himself.

They arrived as planned and without any further searches being conducted en-route, joined the already growing queues for the large ferris wheel, spinning lazily in the morning sun. They staggered themselves so each would be in their own car, and as the wheel spun slowly, so they each embarked in turn with a group of other visitors and sight-seers.

As the cars rose higher, each person took a small metal box, wrapped in crumpled tissue paper, as the carriage was one but last from the exit, so the team casually threw the tissue concealing the metallic box into the small rubbish bin at the far end of the car.

There were two cars with terrorists still in them when the ride stopped unexpectedly, An elderly visitor in a wheelchair was being helped onto the carriage, for which the ride needed to be stopped completely. Precious minutes ticked by, the terrorists already off the ride cast nervous looks at each other. The timers had been set before they'd all got on the ride!

The leader looked at the others around him and said "'C'mon, we need to move for the escape boats. The others will have to take their chance". Without a glance upwards, the team of six moved hurriedly away, towards the Danube.

Up in the farthermost carriage, the terrorist still on board could see the others running away from the scene. Without thinking, he reached into the bin to retrieve the discarded tissue and metallic box, which housed a small explosive device, and smashing one of the ancient windows of the car, threw the box towards the middle of the park.

A split second later, the bomb in the car underneath exploded just as the other 6 cars did in unison. Each a great ball of flame that showered debris onto the waiting queues below, who all started screaming and running away.

The chief of the security operation heard the explosions and saw the smoke rising from the park,

216

where the Ferris Wheel is located. Speaking into his radio quickly he ran for a nearby car and took off at speed for the park.

Meanwhile the 6 surviving members of the Children of WAW were making their way against the tide of people, towards the bridge that spanned the Danube, and their route of escape.

As they neared the bridge ramparts they could see the two promised motor cruisers, engines idling, being held by a single rope looped around one of the jetty poles. Taking the steps two at a time, the team quickly descended and divided onto the 2 waiting boats. They'd hardly jumped aboard when the ropes were cast off and the engines gunned into life as each sped off into the centre of the river.

The leader in the first boat breathed a sigh of relief. They'd actually done it, despite all the security arrangements surrounding the event, striking a dark blow for the Children of WAW against the World's Governments.

The pilot of the boat picked up a radio telephone and after speaking briefly, passed the handset to the leader. The voice at the other end was jubilant, ecstatic, and promised a substantial increase in the final instalment due, before hanging up.

The leader returned the handset to the pilot, steering the boat at speed with utter confidence through the swirling currents where the Danube rejoins itself after splitting either side of Donauinsel.

The two boats were now able to race alongside each other, skipping in each others powerful wash when suddenly both boats exploded into the air, thrown high by the force of powerful explosions that engulfed even the smallest piece of falling wreckage in flames, before falling like rain droplets onto the surface of the Danube, and sinking without a trace.

Chapter 19

19. Heather's Trolley Dash.

Adam had little time to work on his theory that there was perhaps another reason for the Polestarr system, as the hospital had rung to say Heather was being discharged.

Driving the back roads towards Cambridge, and the hospital, he pondered some more on the Polestarr problem. Wednesday was absolutely right about the expense not justifying the means, but what other options did that leave open? What could one person do with a string of Satellites, designed to monitor the weather?

The news came on the radio, and the breaking story of a terrorist explosion in central Vienna. Details were still coming in but it seemed the target had been the antique Ferris Wheel, which had been completely destroyed by multiple blasts.

The Climate talks were still going ahead, but the location had been changed from the intended Palace to an American Air Force Base, nearby.

Climate protestors had been at pains to distance themselves from the organisation that called itself the Children of WAW that had claimed responsibility for the atrocity, repeating that they would only ever partake in peaceful protests.

And in other news.. Adam turned the radio off. Depressing as the news was.

The first inkling that something was wrong happened as Adam drove into the hospital grounds. There were a lot of Police and hospital security people milling around the entrance to the main concourse, and once he'd parked and walked inside, found the inside of the hospital busy with extra security staff.

Walking up to the main reception desk, he announced that he'd come to collect Heather, after being informed she was being discharged.

The receptionist looked both worried and frightened at the same time, as she asked him to take a seat and rang a number quickly. A Police Inspector walked up to him and asked his name and his business. "Look, what's happened here?" Asked Adam. Clearly something was not right.

The Inspector cleared his throat, "ahem, we were alerted by hospital security that a young woman was seen being escorted into a private ambulance. As they neared the rear door, so she called out for help, but was quickly bundled into the back of the ambulance that took off at speed".

"With the help of CCTV footage, we've been able to ascertain that the young woman in question was the same person that you've come to collect, a Miss Heather Lightly".

Adam rocked back on his heels. Heather had been abducted, and it didn't take a million guests to figure out by who. Tek! He cursed that he hadn't foreseen this attempt and asked the Inspector if they had any further information about the route the ambulance had taken?

"We're searching CCTV and ANPR cameras on all routes along their last known direction now, but there are severe gaps in the coverage, and they could already be out of the City or in another vehicle. I suggest you go home sir and wait for us to contact you. If the kidnappers get in touch, if it is a kidnapping, then let us know.

Adam turned and rang back to the car. Calling Jupiter house, he quickly filled in Mate and Wednesday on what had happened. "I'm going to get airborne and widen the search area. Mate, get AMIe to run her own searches of all available footage, and

221

hack the hospital security cameras so we can get a number plate for the ambulance that took Heather".

Adam had driven fast and was already on a deserted country road. "No time like the present AMIe. Deploy flight mode", and as he spoke, he triggered the cars controls to extend the delta shaped flight surfaces from underneath the sides of the car, whilst the nose became even more streamlined and smaller, flaps folded out from the rear of the A-pillars of the car. With a burst of speed from the small rocket that had extended out from the rear of the car, the shiny bronze car took to the skies.

Mate was already heading for the garage and one of the electric bikes, as AMIe fed information to both him and Adam, on her search for the vehicle that had carried Heather away,

"It appears that the vehicle is heading North on the A14 and has just passed onto the newer sections at Bar Hill".

"Got you" whispered Mate as he started the bike and took off up the exit ramp so fast as to manage a controlled wheelie all the way up the ramp, before breaking out onto the dusty track surface and engaging 'trial' mode, rode as the crow flies towards that intersection of road that AMIe had pinpointed.

Price: Polestarr

Adam was also bringing the i8 about in a tight turn, to head at full power towards the newly completed overpass / underpass of the A14 improvements, that helped motorists avoid the narrower streets and bridge over the river at Huntingdon.

The problem was going to be where to set down. The A14 was always notoriously busy, and whilst he wasn't concerned about being spotted, physical landing space was a problem and a vertical landing would waste precious time and momentum in tracking & stopping the vehicle that had Heather.

Inside the ambulance, Heather had been strapped to a wheeled stretcher, which was probably just as well, for the vehicle was driving fast, bouncing and throwing her about on the rickety frame. Every bounce or swerve put pressure on her broken ankle, causing her to grimace, despite the sturdy plaster cast, that covered from her toes to just below her knee.

A surly looking man, dressed in the uniform of an ambulance medic, was preparing a hypodermic syringe, drawing a colourless liquid from a small phial. He pulled her sleeve up roughly and was about to administer the injection when the vehicle bounced and slewed so violently as to make him almost fall of the small seat adjacent to the stretcher.

Jonathan C. Crouch

Reaching out his other hand to steady himself, he tried again but this time Heather was ready for him, and as he moved to inject her, so she quickly shrunk her body & arm backwards, as best the straps would allow, and the injection plunged harmlessly into the thin mattress of the stretcher.

"Stay still" he growled at her, reaching for the same phial to refill the syringe. The ambulance bounced and lurched again, and this time, Heather was able to take in the rear door of the vehicle, and its locking mechanism.

As the medic finished filling the syringe, squirting a little of it up into the air, so Heather made her move. With her hands clinging to the side of the van, she used all her might to pull the rickety stretcher towards the door. A final half-twist of her body and she kicked out at the quick release bar on the back of the ambulance door.

Her guard, thrown off by her quick movements, dropped the syringe and lunged towards her but it was too late. In the spilt-second his attention had been on the small bottle, she'd unlatched the door, that swung back with a deadening 'clunk', locating itself in the safety catches on the outside of the ambulance, to the blaring horns of drivers that swerved to miss the obstacle, and launched herself into the air, still attached to the stretcher.

More horns blaring, and the rush of air past her face as cars swerved to avoid the one-woman missile careening towards them, out of control without any steering or brakes.

The ambulance had been travelling in the middle lane of the road, slightly uphill. Her momentum was carrying her into the overtaking third lane and the crash barriers.

She threw her body weight into making the stretchers wheels turn, and was only successful in diverting away from the crash barriers but heading on an even deadlier path which cut across all three lanes.

More cars, the sound of squealing tyres and brakes, and then an on-coming lorry, flashing headlights and two-tone air horn sounding was upon her. She took an inward sharp breath and passed across the front of the vehicle seconds before it would have collided with her.

The unsteady frame of the bed took off over the embankment and arched serenely down into a collection of bushes and tall grasses. The impact of the fall shattered the flimsy aluminium frame, allowing Heather to slide her restraints free of the bed.

As she stood, dusting herself down, and thanking her lucky stars that nothing was broken, apart from the already plastered ankle, she looked anxiously for her abductees, but neither they nor the ambulance were anywhere to be seen.

She was just contemplating the best direction to head in, not knowing where she was, when a familiar humming reached her ears and moments later, a large motorbike came through the waist tall vegetation towards her. The rider bought the bike to a stop, lifted his visor and spoke "Can I give you a lift back?" Even though the face was a carefully woven mask, she was sure she could see Mate smiling as he said it.

Adam had picked out a small track used by Farm machinery to access the fields, and had just landed, albeit a little bumpily, when Mate reported he'd picked Heather up and was making his way to rendezvous with Adam.

"AMIe, flash Mate our location". "Understood" replied AMIe, sending the coordinates of the i8 to the visor of Mate's helmet. Adam had barely turned the i8 around, when the bike carrying Mate & Heather appeared at the far end of the track and blazed a dusty trail towards him.

Price: Polestarr

Adam rushed from the car to hug Heather, and as he helped her off the bike, she explained how she'd escaped from the bogus ambulance men, and the terrifying white-knuckle ride on the stretcher as she'd made her escape.

"The funny thing is I expected them to have pulled over and come searching for me, but they didn't". "I suspect" replied Adam thinking, "that there orders were to draw as little attention to themselves as possible. I'm pretty sure that they didn't consider your escaping as even a remote possibility".

"What were you and Mate doing so close?" "Ah well, AMIe had hacked every road camera, CCTV and bluetooth enabled private dash-cam and extrapolated this was the most likely route the abductees would take. The next camera they passed on the A14, just over there, confirmed it and of course, Mate and I set off at once".

"Well, thank you for coming to my rescue" Heather replied, with a little pout to suggest that she hadn't needed it in the end. All the same, she was earnestly grateful that the two friends had been so close and would have undoubtedly stopped the bogus ambulance before it had gotten away with her.

"C'mon, climb in and lets get you home", said Adam, half-carrying the limping Heather towards the passenger side of the i8, AMIe already opening the large gull-wing door to allow Heather to slide into the seat, comfortably.

Adam signalled Mate to follow him, and the two set off with their precious passenger, Adam opting for the smoother return by road with Mate shadowing the car, on the lookout for any further trouble.

As it turned out, their fears were unfounded. The journey back was quiet and un-eventful, during which Heather slept, exhausted with the efforts of the day and the pain radiating from her broken ankle, and Adam had time to ponder what Tek's next action would be, and who it would be aimed at.

Chapter 20

20. The End of Jupiter House.

As Adam was driving back home with Heather, contemplating what action Tek would take next, the man himself was in a phone conversation with the driver of the failed ambulance kidnap of Heather Lightly.

Tek's features became darker and more brooding as the call went on, and he finished the call by slamming the handset onto the granite desk in front of him, so hard as to shatter the telephone into small shards of plastic and electronic flotsam.

Pressing a buzzer on the desks intercom, he spoke quickly into the device "Send in my head of security".

A moment passed during which Tek walked back to behind his desk, and seating himself in the large leather chair, turned towards the door as it slid open silently and a large, well built man with the facial features of a large, angry eagle, walked, no not walked, strode with easy purpose to stand in front of Tek's desk, hands clasped behind his back.

"Those bungling idiots in the UK allowed Ms Lightly to escape and now she's back with Dr Price. I want you" he emphasised the point by jabbing a stubby digit at the man "to get over to England now and take care of this situation once and for all. Price and his friends cannot be allowed to continue their investigations into my organisation, understood?".

The man hadn't moved or shown any emotion during Tek's tirade, but now that he'd finished speaking, he merely nodded and with a swift turnabout, remarkably light of foot for such a large man, strode quickly out of the office, leaving Tek to gloat of his own brilliance, whilst nursing a large whiskey in his over-sized hands, like a gambler, shuffling dice in his palm.

Captain Andrew Green had served with the Marines, working his way up the ranks from a lowly cadet, when he joined the Royal Navy at sixteen. The SAS had recruited him after he'd been mentioned and commended in a field report for single-handedly taking out six of the enemy and carrying his unconscious comrade to a safe rendezvous point, all with a broken leg.

But political alliances had changed and Governments had become more obsessed with their own power and brilliance and the forces, once deemed necessary to protect democracy, were now being shut down or restricted to diplomatic bag exchanges.

He'd gone private and handed in his commission before being pushed. He'd seen what that had done to some of his fellow comrades, burnt-out alcoholics (or worse), sleeping rough, with no purpose or goal, and no orders to follow either.

The leg had been expertly repaired by the Navy's top surgeons and now only the occasional twinge bothered him when it was especially cold. That is too say his leg had been painful every day since his arrival at the North Pole headquarters. The UK would seem positively tropical by comparison, and he boarded the small jet with no small measure of satisfaction.

***

Everyone was settled in large comfy chairs in the lounge of Jupiter House, the room lit with soft lighting from multiple lamps, providing a restful ambience against the darkening skies outside.

Wednesday had been so pleased to see Heather back safely and had immediately whisked her into the living room, fussing over her with cushions and pillows, so that she was half sat up, with the broken ankle raised slightly on its on pillow.

AMIe was projecting a large 3D image of the Earth, slowly spinning in real time, generated from a cleverly concealed section of the coffee table, with various coloured contours flowing around the land-masses.

They'd all watched the evening news earlier, which had as its main story, the terrorist attach in Vienna, and the deaths of the suspected perpetrators in a separate boating incident. Police and forensics were still working diligently at both sites in order to try and gather some evidence for the Police to follow-up on.

Adam had proposed that the terrorists - the Children of WAW - were in fact a small hub working on the instructions of Tek, to provide impetuous to the demands for change from businesses and relax the complicated mining and extraction rules currently in place.

No Government wanted a repeat of the events in Paris and now Vienna on their own soil, and you could hardly blame them, given the global unrest as civilisation seemed to be breaking down, and law & order took more and more of a bashing from groups intent on igniting civil unrest.

If Tek was involved with the Children of WAW group, and AMIe had presented some very interesting findings concerning phone calls from the boats moments before they exploded, and a complicated trail of phone masts and relays that had ended up at the location of the Mountain HQ at the North Pole, despite the attempts to throw any would be followers off of the real origin of the phone call.

"Which just goes to prove, in my mind, that Tek is unhinged and dangerously so. The question is what do we do about it?"

"Couldn't we just go to the authorities with all we've unearthed and get them to send in plane loaded with bombs and blow the whole place sky-high?" Asked Heather with Wednesday nodding her agreement to the plan.

"It's a nice idea" replied Mate, his synthesised voice sounding resigned, "but Tek has most of the World's Governments in his hands by now. They'll no sooner order a military strike on him than keep an electoral promise".

"Mate's right" added Adam. "No, if action is needed then its down to us four here to see it through".

"Five" said AMIe, as the Wednesday helped Heather up from the sofa, and the three of them turned in for the night, Mate's suit slowly deflating as they left the room and AMIe turned off the lights.

The following morning was damp & misty. An early sign that Autumn was approaching. The usual blue skies were replaced with a more sombre, blanket of grey cloud, and the morning air had an unusual nip to it.

Inside the house as the occupants stirred, AMIe was already controlling the under-floor heating to give a pleasant warmth to the living rooms, and after each had showered or bathed, Heather with her cast-wearing leg hung over the side of the bath to keep dry, they all met in the kitchen for breakfast.

Amongst the usual fried breakfast, pancakes and cereals on offer, was the addition of porridge, to which Wednesday helped herself, sprinkling blueberries and mango pieces onto the steaming warm bowl.

Adam was already finished, scanning a tablet, information flashing upwards with each swipe, as Heather also limped in on crutches, to join them, declining anything more than black coffee and toast, which she spread liberally with thick honey from a local farm apiary.

Mate still hadn't materialised yet. His suit was still laid out, deflated, on a sofa in the living room.

Heather asked Adam about Mate's erratic materialisation periods, which seemed to be growing more unpredictable as the days passed. Adam acknowledged he too was worried about the "unstableness of Mate's molecular structure" and voiced his opinion that the sooner they could get a break from their present assignment, he would endeavour to conduct some serious studies and experiments, to see if Mate's condition could be improved.

Wednesday then asked "what sort of experiments can you do, without harming Mate further?"

"I don't know" replied Adam, "but that's what we're going to find out, treading as cautiously as we can. The one certainty is that, for the moment, the suit appears to be working still. There is the matter of his increased capabilities, like when he expanded suddenly to take out the security patrol in the snow, before we escaped. What else mighty he be capable of?" Adam left the question hanging in the air as Wednesday turned the conversation to how Heather was feeling, and they continued until breakfast was a finished and the three headed for the underground Lab.

Heather was sat at a small desk, specially heightened for a wheelchair user to sit comfortably at, with a small laptop, talking on the phone that was tucked under one ear against her shoulder, as she continued to scribble notes.

Wednesday was working at the main weather pattern work station with its 3D virtual model of the ocean currents and temperatures, whilst Adam was in the garage area, working on repairs to the i8, aided by small robotic arms, refitting panels and components with precision and speed.

AMIe announced that the car needed a complete re-boot that would take much of the buildings systems off-line for several minutes. Once everyone was finished with what they were working on, AMIe started the process, shutting down various systems normally automated, visible on a large screen as the status bars sank to zero.

Passing critical points of low-power, a soft warning hooting could be heard which Adam quickly moved to silence.

On the surface, the houses lights flickered and went to emergency lighting mode, as Tek's head of security, Green watched through powerful binoculars from the neighbouring hill. Having already reconnoitred the area the night before.

From his vantage point, he'd see the three move from the dining room into the middle of the house, but they hadn't emerged for some time. Probably a basement of some kind not on the buildings architect plans, he thought to himself.

No matter, the small portable rocket launcher laying beside him, was often referred to as a Tank Buster, and would obliterate the house and any basement beneath in a single stroke.

Tek's plans had been to subtle, to abstract, to abduct one of Price's friends. The man was both a menace and persistent, and could even now be working on ways to get to Tek.

Without taking his eyes from the field binoculars, he reached out his right hand and patted the tubular rocket launcher, almost with affection. Dr Price wouldn't be bothering them for very much longer.

He checked his watch, 10 minutes until the cargo airline he'd callously selected would be in view and beginning its descent, for landing at the nearby Stansted Airport.

An all-out direct strike on the home of Dr Price would have been too suspicious but an airliner crashing to earth, well that was a different thing altogether, and by the time the investigation had concluded the cause of the crash, Tek's plans would be giving the authorities bigger things to worry about.

He checked his watch again, as just at the moment the sound of a multi-jet engined airliner could be heard in the distance. With the aid of computer simulations, he'd been able to calculate the exact moment he needed to strike in order to precipitate the airliner crashing to Earth on top of Price's house.

His target was the foremost engine on the left wing of the aircraft as it moved right to left across the sky in front of him. Picking up the small rocket launcher, he extended the fibreglass tube to its full two metre length and folding out the cross-haired laser sight, trained the weapon on the unsuspecting aircraft.

His watch was counting down the seconds and at the precisely calculated moment, he squeezed the trigger unleashing the missile towards the airplane, its fiery, smoky trail billowing out from behind as the rocket sped upwards to its intended target.

Down below, AMIe was still re-booting the systems, and Price, Heather and Wednesday were completely unaware of the drama unfolding above them.

On the flight deck, the Captain had just disengaged the automatic pilot as he and the co-pilot readied the

238

plane for its final approach and landing at Stansted Airport, now minutes away.

The small but lethal missile struck the airliner exactly as planned, as the whole left wing disintegrated in flames, sending the plane into an uncontrollable downward spiral. The co-pilot was shouting wildly into the radio, while the Captain fought with non-existent flight control surfaces. Most of the cabins electronics had failed but back-up gauges all told the same story.

Whispering a quick, heart-felt farewell to his family, into the microphone which he knew would be encapsulated in the recovered flight recorders, he braced himself for the approaching impact as the ground spun upwards towards them. He could make out a small village, houses & hillsides, pretty gardens and even swimming pools. In the last few seconds, he saw a modern looking, low white structure, slightly isolated from the surrounding homes. Perhaps they were out?

Down in the Lab, the whole world seemed to shake as even the emergency lights flickered off and a thick layer of dust filled the air, followed by the dull sound of a large explosion. Adam grabbed a torch as he interrupted the i8's reboot and bought AMIe back on-line.

Running down the short tunnel towards the lift back to the house, he was met with nothing but chalky rubble, where the lift shaft had once been.

Turning back, he checked Wednesday and Heather were alright, as the lights came back on, and jumping in the i8, drove up the exit ramp at speed. Bursting out onto the ground track, he spun the car about and stopping, leapt from the car to look towards the house.

His eyes couldn't believe what they were seeing. A large tail fin from an airliner was standing upright where once the house has stood. The back section of the jet was on fire. Everything else was in pieces, some burning, others smoking as already the wail of sirens could be heard approaching in the distance.

The heat was intense from the burning fuel and as the smoke billowed out across the fields, so the first fire engine arrived and deployed fire-fighters and hoses. Five more engines quickly joined their comrades and they fought to douse the fuel-fed flames.

A small knot of firemen had already fought their way to the wreckage but it was obvious to everyone that there were no survivors. Villagers had also rushed to the scene, some filming on mobile phones whilst others had come more prepared to help, carrying blankets and first aid kits.

The posh modern house that had once stood there was now just rubble & glass, with scraps of furniture flapping in the breeze, the only sign that someone had once lived there.

A large black Range Rover had pulled up and several suited men climbed out, followed by a rather elderly gent, seemingly out of place in his bowler hat and cane. A knee-length black coat pulled tight against the Autumn chill.

The old man moved forward to speak with the Fire officer in charge. They exchanged a few brief words but the fire-chiefs body language spoke volumes. There were no survivors from the airplane or the house, if anyone had been at home at the time.

Jonathan C. Crouch

Chapter 21

21. Retreat to Cairn Castle.

Adam returned to the i8 and drove back down the ramp & into the garage area.

Wednesday & Heather were both in tears. AMIe had re-started all systems and a live camera stream was showing the devastation above them.

"Oh those poor people on the plane" Wednesday had sobbed.

"I know" replied Adam solemnly. "The question is, was it an accident or deliberate?"

Heather looked at him incredulously "you can't mean someone planned for this to happen?"

"Well it does seem almost too coincidental that a regular flight just happens to crash right in top of us. The precision is almost computer like. Like you, I struggle to believe it was deliberate but I just don't know".

Running to a nearby computer console, Adam asked AMIe to show the aircrafts flight path. As

AMIe played back the last few seconds of the flight, so it careened wildly and fell to earth. "Do we have any surveillance footage?"

"Negative, the systems were all off-line at the precise moment the accident occurred".

"See if you can get anything from nearby security cameras, anything. I don't care what you have to hack into, we need to see the final moments before the plane crashed".

"Working" replied AMIe, as the screen was replaced with a blue circular graphic to show AMIe was working on something.

Wednesday had gotten control of her emotions and her and Heather had begun clearing the debris from the tables and desks. A large booming noise was heard and the ceiling creaked and groaned as beams and panelling sagged downwards.

"It's possible the structural damage is worse than we thought" said Adam. "I think its probably safest if we think about evacuating the area for now".

"Where can we go?" Asked Heather.

"You remember my old Scottish retreat?" Replied Adam, "I kept it on and have been working on & off to restore it to some usefulness. I think we can all fit in".

"And what about all our work here?" Asked Wednesday.

"AMIe can quickly transfer herself to any location, and there is equipment already there to work with. We'll just need to replace personal belongings and anything that was in the house".

He spun around on the desk stool he'd been perched on to type at a keyboard. "AMIe, transfer everything to Cairn Castle, and get the castle and labs up & running will you".

"We can't all fit in the i8, but there's a electric powered Range Rover at the back of the garage area, we'll use instead." Setting the security protocols in place to completely seal off the cave once they'd exited, the three climbed into the gleaming silver SUV and for the last time, Adam drove up the ramp and out onto the dusty farm track.

They stopped at a large out of town, shopping village, where they bought new clothes, toiletries and food & drink for the journey. They stopped again on the border for a quick rest-room stop, before setting off. The day was already turning dark, when the got their first glimpse of the mountain peaks of the

Highlands, and stopping again, to picnic at the side of the road, set off for the final leg of the drive to Loch Earn.

With a certain sense of Deja-vu, Adam pulled onto the car park of the Loch Earn Inn. The still waters of the Loch itself shimmered in the brief patches of moonlight that struck the surface as clouds scudded across the night sky. The air was crisp and laden with the scent of pine and damp moss, as the three stretched before heading into the welcoming reception hall.

A young girl was on the desk, typing furiously into her mobile phone, when the three approached the desk. Instantly she put down the phone and smiled in welcome. "Good evening and welcome to The Loch Earn Inn. How may I help you?"

"We'd like three rooms please, just for tonight" explained Adam, continuing "we're visiting friends further North but its gotten too late to continue the journey tonight".

"That's not a problem" replied the girl "if you'll all just sign in here" and speaking as she turned, took three huge old fashioned keys from the wooden shelf behind her.

Price: Polestarr

"Now I just need to take your card details for a wee deposit, and you can charge anything to the rooms. Breakfast is served from 7 until 10am. You'll find there's plenty of hot water and fresh towels in your rooms, which are at the top of the landing, to your left".

Wishing the three a sweet goodnight, Adam, Heather and Wednesday climbed the stairs and located their rooms, exactly as the receptionist had promised. With promises to catch up in the morning, Adam suggested they all turn-in for the night. The mountain air with its scent of heather, worked its magic on weary travellers and quickly all three were fast asleep.

The next morning dawned bright and sunny, giving the mountains and Loch a fresh, appealing look. From their rooms, the three travellers could gaze out onto the nearest mountain side and if they leant out of the windows ever-so-slightly, could see the outline of Cairn Castle high up on the neighbouring ridge.

Breakfast was a grand affair, served by the same pretty receptionist. As she served porridge (with salt) "there's cream, sugar and syrups on the table", moving expertly between tables collecting dishes, pouring drinks and chatting with the few other guests.

It was only as she was serving the full fried breakfasts to Adam's table that he asked after the landlord from his previous stay. "My Uncle's away and asked me to take care of the Inn for him".

Smiling, she turned away to tend to other guests that had just arrived in the dining room. "I stayed here once before" commented Adam "and so I believe did you Heather" he finished, with a raised eyebrow.

They had spoken little about the atrocity that had occurred at Jupiter House, hastening their departure, each lost in their own thoughts as the spectacular scenery had rolled past the cars windows.

Now they were all walking the track that led to the castle, littered with boulders and chunks of rock from the explosion of the castle, which it was originally believed had claimed Adam's life.

But here and there, nature was returning as it always does, and the re-affirming belief was a tonic for their tortured thoughts, grim as they had been, the sunny day combined with the scenery, worked its magic and refreshed them all. Gave them hope that the battle wasn't lost.

Once up closer to the castle, they could see that some limited building work had taken place. The previous guest wing still fractured away from the main walls of the castle, still leant out at a crazy angle, propped up by an intricate support fashioned out of scaffolding poles.

Reaching the front door, set within a portcullis looking decorative framework of stone & timber, Adam unlocked it and the three walked into the hallway. Once a beautifully preserved & historically accurate depiction of the once grand entrance, it was now much more up to date with cosy lighting and large sweeping sofa's arranged around an open fire pit in the middle of the floor.

The room was circular with the outer edge 2 steps up from the main floor, to form a kind of open corridor around the circumference of the room, where steps led to smooth timber doorways. "Guest rooms and kitchen-cum-dining area" Adam explained.

Taking a small key from his pocket, he crossed to the furthest point from the entrance and pulled aside a small hanging tapestry to reveal a steel door. He unlocked a small keypad on the wall, and pressed a sequence of buttons on the simple pad. There was a slight hiss as the door opened, revealing a short corridor, which ended in another similar door.

"An airlock" marvelled Wednesday, taking in the room and the contrast of the interior of the corridor they were now entering.

"Yes" replied Adam smiling. "This ensures a permanent barrier between the labs and the outside World. Come, let me give you a brief tour".

Adam led Wednesday and Heather through the small, but perfectly equipped complex of rooms. Small workstations with all the latest computer technology and interactive virtual headsets and projection equipment.

The largest room was an almost exact replica of the main Lab that had been at Jupiter house, and as Adam flicked on the lights, so AMIe's voice spoke out to welcome them.

"I've finished my surveillance scan of all the footage I could find on the flight that ended exploding on top of us. I think you'll find the montage of images on the main screen quite compelling, if a little disturbing to watch".

Without waiting for an answer, AMIe ran the footage she un-earthed. Around the main screen were several smaller screens, all showing different angles of the same event. Most were captures from people's mobile phones, whilst a few were from misaligned

CCTV that happened to be pointing upwards rather than downwards. Car dash-cam footage and even web-cams from bird boxes on the St Swithun's Church tower. The clearest / best footage had been cleverly spliced to give a 3D frame by frame depiction of events.

"Here we can see the flight progressing normally" began AMIe. "The Captain is just switching off the auto-pilot, in readiness for starting the landing procedure at London Stansted airport." The next minute there was a blinding explosion as the left engine was engulfed in flames. "Here you can see the point of the fatal explosion. At first glance an engine fault, but, if we wind back frame-by-frame, we see this".

The screen showed a small object making contact with the engine. The same frames again but enlarged, showed a small cylindrical device hitting the engine cowling. "A missile attack" said Adam. "Indeed" replied AMIe. "I've managed to extrapolate where it was fired from, given the prevailing weather, angle of ascent and range of such a missile".

A 3D map of terrain around Jupiter House now rose out of the central projector table. "You can see the location of the house, and now", said AMIe, "the aircraft flying over head. Working the angles backwards, we see this small copse the likely location from which the missile was fired.

I've managed to get access to the preliminary report and the traces of chemicals and metals that have been analysed so far, lead to this", a picture of a small hand-held launch tube appeared on the main screen, code name 'Tank Buster'. As the specification for both the missile and the launcher scrolled upwards, whilst the image changed to show the weapon being test-fired in a variety of scenarios by military personnel.

"Someone took down an entire jet, causing the death of many just to kill me" Adam snarled it and then immediately staggered backwards as the horror of what he'd just uttered over-whelmed him.

Heather caught him and swung him around to a nearby chair that he thankfully fell onto. His head hung low in the utter shame of the lives lost because of him.

"It's not your fault" said Wednesday softly, "The finger that pulled the trigger and the person that ordered it are the ones responsible". He took her had and lifting his head, tears running down his face, nodded his understanding of what she'd said. "The question is" said Heather "who?"

Price: Polestarr

"I've a pretty good idea" said Adam wiping his face on his sleeve and standing to walk over to the computer table. "Winston Tek!"

"Tek?" Replied Heather "why?"

"Because I was getting to close, joining up the dots, endangering whatever operation he's involved in. Someone truly de-ranged devised and carried out the bringing down of that jet but the ultimate aim of silencing me was ordered by Tek. Of that I'm sure".

The video playback was still rolling; now showing footage from a helicopter or drone, circling the remains of the house and the crash site, recognisable bits of aircraft strewn amongst the buildings rubble remains. A suitcase here, a seat there, and bits of engine or wing.

"What about Mate" Heather suddenly exclaimed. "Oh my gosh, we forget about Mate".

"Don't worry" soothed Adam, "Mate was fine. Remember he wasn't in his suit at the time of the strike. Hopefully, he'll locate and join us here before too long".

"Does he have a suit he can use here?" Asked Wednesday.

Jonathan C. Crouch

"Yes, I've kitted the quarters and workshop out with a variety of suits for him. Upgrades on what he's been using previously with one or two modifications I hope he'll find useful.

C'mon, let's head back to the living area and get some dinner. Meanwhile, I've a quick phone call to make to and old friend".

The bowler hat wearing old gentleman that had arrived at Jupiter House and talked with the fire chief, was sat behind that oddly out of place, elegantly carved French desk, devoid of anything except a phone and a sheaf of files, the old gent had been looking through slowly.

The phone rang. Curious because it was a direct call from the outside and there were only a handful of people that had that number. That it displayed as 'unknown caller' was another mystery. All this he pondered in the time it took to reach for the handset and lift it to his ear.

"Hello?" He spoke tentatively.

"It's Dr Adam Price sir", came the voice at the other end. Adam continued quickly "I don't have much time but I just wanted to assure you I was alive and well. We all are" he added. "I've studied the data and reports on the remains found at the site of my

254

former home, and we've concluded the airplane was bought down by a hand-held rocket, called a Tank-Buster. We've pinpointed the location it was fired from and I'm sending that data to you now. Hopefully you'll be able to get a trace on whoever pulled the trigger.

There's something else. We believe that Winston Tek was behind the order to kill me. I think it was because I, with Wednesday and Heather, are onto something with the whole Polestarr operation".

"That's a serious allegation. Do you have any proof?"

"Not yet" replied Adam, "Not concrete, no. But I had to warn you to be on your guard for anything unexpected or out of the ordinary. Whatever Tek is planning, I think its nearing completion.

One thing I do have is evidence linking Tek with the Children of WAW group. An intercepted phone call that although well disguised, was originally made from a location in the Artic circle, to the boats the terrorists were escaping on up the Danube, before they exploded".

"We'll look into that some more" replied the Old man, cradling the phone's handset, he added "it's good to hear you're all safe and well, but you're not going to tell me where you are?" "Not for now Sir. Well, goodbye" and the line went dead.

The old gentleman replaced the handset on its resting hook, and leaned back in his padded chair, placing his hands together, fingertips outstretched like he was praying for divine inspiration or at lest an insight into what was really happening, from the heavens themselves.

Chapter 22

22. Better Believed Dead.

Adam, Heather and Wednesday were finishing their evening meal when AMIe alerted them that Mate's energy signature was detected in the vicinity of one of the guest rooms.

The three rushed to the indicated rooms doorway and Adam opened the door carefully. On the large bed was a recognisable suit laid out for its occupant to appear in.

As they watched, so the one piece suit with its clever high collar and hood concealing the fact there wasn't a face, just a dark cloth, started to fill out.

As it continued to expand, so the small set of lights on the suits collar flickered and the bars grew steadily, lighting one after the other until all 5 little bars were present. Mate's voice echoed around the room, "Hi everyone. I take it we're not in Jupiter anymore?".

"No" replied Adam.

"We were forced to take a little Scottish holiday" added Heather. "A small matter of someone bringing an airliner down directly onto Jupiter House. The explosion was enough to weaken the underpinning structure of the caves underneath, where we all were at the time of the crash, thank fully".

"It was Tek" finished Adam, "and he's a man we've all got to stop now, somehow.

"But Tek believes you're all dead?" Said Mate and I should know, there's certain advantages to being believed dead. For one, nobody is looking for you anymore".

"You know you might be right" replied Adam, "and that gives me an idea about how we can play this. Gather round everyone" and he launched into his plans.

Tek was strutting around his office impatiently. A radio call had told him to expect for the arrival of Green, back from his adventures in Cambridgeshire. Of course, Tek had seen the airliner crash on the news and its precise location and put two and two together immediately.

Now he was impatient to see the man and hear his account first-hand before he decided on how he was going to handle the man whose tendency to violence out-matched even his own lust for power by any means possible, sometimes.

There was a smart knock at the door and as he muttered "come in", so Tek seated himself behind the larger 'power' desk. Green walked in and stood, impassive, before his boss.

"Mission accomplished sir. Dr Price and his friends have been eliminated".

"Yes and in such a manner, it's a wonder the whole security forces aren't already knocking on my front door".

"To the wider media and security forces, it will look like another airline disaster or if they do think there's more to it, then other countries or terrorist organisations will be blamed. No-one will come knocking on your door".

The man was smart, arrogant almost cocky. Tek didn't have to like the man to appreciate the job he did, but nonetheless, this latest instance was both callous and careless.

"Well don't unpack. I've got another job for you. This time in Scotland. The jets already standing by. You'll get all the details once you arrive at the usual location". With that, Green exited the room smartly and left Tek to ponder his next move. Picking up his

259

phone, he dialled a number, that was answered almost before it had chance to ring. Tek spoke quickly "our friend is just taking off. See to it that it doesn't arrive".

Almost poetic, thought Tek, replacing the receive slowly. The man's demise was going to be of the same fashion, that had made his dismissal necessary in the first place.

***

As Adam had finished outlining his plans, so Heather spoke "Just one question. How do we get to Vandenberg? The i8's still in the caves beneath Jupiter House and more than likely buried under tonnes of rubble".

Adam smiled, "You don't think I have another car already here? Let me show you, and rising, he led the way back through the airlock, only this time instead of walking through the doorway at the other end, he pressed a small button on his watch and the whole corridor turned 90 degrees to face a new doorway. Stepping through it, they all found themselves in a large natural cavern.

"This must be incredibly close to the surface" said Mate.

"It is. The grounds too rocky and hard to excavate out more than a few feet. What we have here is a
260

natural cave on the hillside that I've just had the front covered over".

In the middle of the cave stood a gleaming i8 supercar, similar to the one they'd last seen at Jupiter House but this was a deep metallic ruby red colour, sitting on thick black alloy wheels. The roofline looked different and Adam explained that this model had a t-bar style roof, so occupants could eject straight out rather than the earlier method of the side doors. The weight saving had been used to strengthen the frame and add one of two extra special features.

"And we're taking it for a spin?" Asked Wednesday.

"You and I are travelling to Vandenberg, while Mate makes his own way there. Heather, I need you to get in touch with your newspaper chums. I need to know what other pies Tek has his sticky fingers in. I think there's a connection, if we can just join the dots. Also, his family background, early years stuff".

Heather said she'd try and get as much information as she could while they were gone. "Right stand back everybody, Wednesday if you'd take your seat" said Adam, as he crossed to the other side of the car, which was already turning to face the cave opening - a steel door that was folding back on itself like bi-folding doors opening. A small ramp appeared out of the floor, rising upwards towards the opening, while

261

behind the car another blast hatch had opened, to give the jet engine something to push against.

Adam had already initiated the flight mode and the car's delta wing shape arrangement was unfolding from the underneath of the car, whilst stabilising tail fins folded out of the rear pillars, and a tail protruded from the bottom of the rear bumper. The reflective bronzed glass made the interior impenetrable.

"All set AMIe?" Asked Adam of the car.

"All set" replied the dependable AMIe. "Launch power at your discretion".

"Hit it" replied Adam, enjoying the sudden burst of speed as the car shot out of the opening, wheels barely missing the newly grown gorse and heather bushes, and up into the fiery evening sky, before becoming lost in the brilliant red and orange hues of the approaching sunset.

Adam turned the car onto a course that took them on an arc over the Atlantic, sometimes referred to as a 'Great Circle route', towards the East coast of North America. From there, it was a shorter jump over to the West Coast of California and Vandenberg Air Force Base, where Tek had manufactured and launched his satellites from.

Price: Polestarr

With AMIe at the controls, their cruising height well above the normal height of transatlantic airlines, Adam and Wednesday could sit back and relax. Wednesday was recounting the first visit with Heather to Jupiter House, and although it had only been a week, it felt like the whole Summer, so much had happened to her.

"And the advances you've allowed me to make in my own weather studies. If Tek's satellite system is believed to be false by the rest of the World, then my ocean model should provide a valuable tool".

Adam replied that he was glad to be of assistance, and felt he'd put her in more danger, rather than protected her. "If you're work does become the leading guide for weather and climate studies, them I'm glad".

The powerful car was able to make the flight in the same time as Concorde had been able to make the transatlantic flight, and it seemed to Wednesday that she'd hardly got comfy before AMIe was announcing their arrival at the East coast of America. Slowly the Nova Scotia coastline came into view, its island like outline showing vividly against the blue sea. Even the wake of large ships was still visible at this height.

AMIe lowered their height a little and pointed the i8 towards Vandenberg. The flight across America giving the two occupants time to marvel at both the natural and man-made spectacles of the great country. A little under two hours later, AMIe announced they were loosing height in preparation for a landing on the outskirts of Vandenberg.

Adam, took over the controls, as they flew into the cover of the darkness of an early evening, heading for the unused road he'd landed on once before.

As the wheels touched the ground, so the car quickly gathered in its wings and rear flight surfaces, so that by the time the interior controls had reverted to their road going car configuration, the outer appearance of the super car was just that and no more.

AMIe was projecting their route on the main navigation display. Adam had been wary of attracting the attention of any of Tek's goons, wanting to avoid any trouble, especially on foreign soil.

But it seemed his fears were unfounded as they cruised quietly into the edges of the town and rolled silently into the car park of a comfortable motel.

AMIe had already called ahead and booked their rooms, so it was just a matter of checking in and collecting their keys.

Price: Polestarr

As they walked across the grounds towards the guest lodges, it suddenly occurred to them both that they hadn't eaten for several hours. A small unassuming restaurant, its neon sign proclaiming they were open, lighting its own small parking lot in a garish red light, beckoned and as one, they both turned towards the welcoming sign and the smell of french fries cooking.

A cheerful waitress showed them to a booth on the end wall, and handed them large laminated menus, designed to look like old wild-west wanted posters.

Every dish had been given a similarly characteristic name. As Adam scanned down the list, sun-downers burger and apache platter made him smile. Wednesday was also finding the menu "cute" and commented that it seemed you could have anything, as long as it came with fries.

In the end, she decided on the homestead chicken whilst Adam chose the desperado chilli burger and a beer for both of them.

As their drinks arrived, along with a basket of sweet bread rolls, warm and freshly baked, the two sat back and discussed their respective fields of scientific work. Wednesday was keen to know when Adam had decided to become a scientific recluse.

"When I realised the full potential of my fusion energy experiments and how that could easily be perverted into the most destructive weapon, I knew that other parties were going to be coming after me and my invention.

I'd accumulated enough money to fund the setting up of the Lab in Scotland and the larger working & living area under the hills of Barnsdale. My experiments and engineering tinkering kept me occupied and out of trouble, until Mehat came for me".

"You've sacrificed so much" she said, taking his hand.

"I still can't forgive myself for what happened to Mate, and now the danger I've put you and Heather in".

Their meals arrived and they ate in silence. Their reflections in the window showed faces so deep in thought, they might have been a million miles away.

Chapter 23

23. Wednesday's Bad Habits.

The morning broke unusually warm for the time of year, and although the trees had started shedding their brown leaves, there was no strong gusty wind from the Pacific to dislodge them from their branches.

Old men sat on porch benches dotted along the planked sidewalks of the shops, and muttered that they'd never known such a mild start to the Autumn, only to be corrected by an Octogenarian of the great Winter of '48 "when the snow had fallen for 7 days solid, cutting them off from the rest of World.

Adam emerged from his room and took in a deep lungful of the air, laced with sea salt and the fallen leaves. It was not unpleasant.

Wednesday appeared from her neighbouring room, and locking the door behind her, walked over to where Adam was stood. "So today we hopefully get some answers" she said simply. "Yes" replied Adam "and if my suspicions are right, I'm not looking forward to them being confirmed".

"C'mon, lets go" he said waving towards the car that stood a little way off, a group of men and young boys crowding around the foreign sports car, gleaming in its Ruby Red paint, matching perfectly the reddening leaves of the trees arounds them.

As the crowd parted and dispersed a little at the 'blips' of the alarm de-activating, Adam and Wednesday opened the doors and quickly climbed in, eager to avoid any prolonged discussion with the locals, lest they should tip-off someone at the Tek offices there were foreign strangers in town.

Taking the road to the former Air Force base, Adam had already placed their visitor badges on the dashboard as they rolled to a silent stop at the Base's security gate.

A guard, one Adam didn't recognise from his last visit, approached the car cautiously, his rifle slung across his left hand, right hand gripping the automatic rifle's butt and trigger. Bending down as Adam wound down the electric window, the guard quickly took in the stylish interior of the car and Wednesday sat in the opposite passenger seat.

Price: Polestarr

"May I enquire who you're here to see?" Asked the guard mechanically, almost bored. "Yes" replied Adam. "Myself and my colleague are here from the London Times newspaper, to write a piece on the birthplace of the rocket age and America's reach towards the stars". He hoped he sounded gushing enough, as the Guard checked his visitor roster.

"I don't have anyone matching your description or coming from your paper on my visitor list. I'm afraid I can't admit you". "Oh that's a real shame" said Wednesday sweetly, leaning over Adam slightly to be in the guards line of sight. Mr Tek will be so disappointed, especially after meeting with our editor only last week, and arranging these passes for us" she fingered the flap of printed plastic on its shiny chrome clip, attached to her jackets lapel.

At the sound of Tek's name, the guard visibly straightened. "Oh well if its all been organised with Mr Tek's people, then I'm sure its OK to let you in. You'll find their offices at the end of Vanguard drive, straight on and left at the top. Have a good day y'all" he threw in as Adam settled for just nudging the accelerator and the i8 moved forward under the still-rising security barrier.

"Nice touch" remarked Adam smiling. "I seem to be picking up some of Heather's journalistic traits" she laughed back, as the two continued to drive in the direction of Tek's offices.

Rather than park in the main car park, Adam settled for pulling up under the shade of an evergreen tree on the boundary wall of Tek's office building. Climbing out, they both quickly looked around them, lest they'd been spotted, before moving quickly towards the rear of the building, taking notice of the security cameras, as they went.

It was a small, un-assuming doorway that Adam had seen on his last visit and if he remembered correctly, led to a short corridor, before entering into the main foyer. "With any luck, their should only be a skeleton staff at the weekends" he whispered to Wednesday. "Where's Mate?" She whispered back. "I'm hoping he's already arrived and in Tek's offices, disarming the security. Lets see" and as he spoke, Adam turned to his wrist-watch - a digital device - and pressed the two side buttons simultaneously. A small radar like wave was emanating outwards from the 6 o'clock position on the watch face, in graduating lines of faintness. As he moved in a slow semi-circle, the wrist held in front of him, so there was a quiet blip and corresponding blue dot appeared on the farthest reach of the watch face.

"He's here" smiled Adam.

"That's a handy device" replied Wednesday to which Adam replied "I figured it might come in useful to know where Mate was. Especially when he's materialised but invisible".

The two walked stealthily but there was no need. Adam's assertion that the building would be practically empty due to it being the weekend proved to be correct, and they were quickly at the door to Tek's office, without being detected.

Adam was about to try the door, when the handle turned slowly and the door opened a crack, as if someone was peering out.

Seeing it was Adam and Wednesday, the door opened fully to allow the pair in, before closing silently, the slight click of the catch the only sound.

"You made it alright?" Asked Adam of the empty office. A distorted crackling, like that of a badly tuned radio, began to rise in volume, gaining clarity as it rose, until Mate's distinct voice could be heard, via Adam's watch.

"I arrived ages ago" Mate boasted. "The whole building appears to be empty and full automated, with only a minimal crew of technicians down in the satellite control bunker. I've been roaming the halls, checking out some of the other rooms, mostly small meeting rooms, before I came back to Tek's office and tried to access some of his more protected computer files".

"Any luck?" Asked Adam.

"Some" said Mate. "There's a lot of technical schematics and drawings of electronic circuits, I assume for the Satellites. There's also blueprints for the Artic base. You know, that structure is massive and appears to be fully self-supportive. The reactor is, as you'd guessed, far below in the depths of the sea, connected by a steel umbilical tunnel".

"How are you able to use a computer?" Asked Wednesday, still getting used to talking to thin air.

"Mate can concentrate his elements to produce a solid form. Enough to type with two fingers or move a computer mouse anyway". Adam continued "you say these technical schematics are for the satellites? Perhaps we'd better start by looking at those in more detail".

As various technical draughts moved across the large computer screen, Adam was struck by the simplicity of many of the designs. Tek's people had really done an amazing job, albeit for less than strictly good intentions, or perhaps they were being fooled along with everybody else?

Price: Polestarr

One drawing though seemed odd and out of place when compared with the other circuitry and wiring drawings. It took Adam a minute to realise that it was only half a drawing. Scanning quickly through the remaining files, he found another seemingly unfinished diagram. Merging the two drawings together, completed the circuit diagram, and as its meaning dawned on Adam, he quickly took a photo of the document, before shutting the computers down and instructing Mate and Wednesday that they were leaving immediately.

"What have you found?" Asked a worried Wednesday as Mate too, voiced his concerns at the sudden decision to leave.

"If I'm right" replied Adam, "then this schematic is what the Polestarr program is really all about. A very elaborate and expensive smoke-screen, even with the data manipulation, to stop anyone from digging any further and discovering the real truth".

"What truth is that?" Asked Mate.

"Tek is quite mad, and intends to destroy half the planet by sending the two super-powers into a nuclear confrontation. For all we know, it might have already begun".

He had just begun to move towards the door, when the handle started turning. Someone was coming in!

Wednesday dived behind one of the large sofa's, while Adam took a seat and tried to look as innocent as possible.

It was Tek's personal assistant, backing into the room, holding the door open with her bottom, as she fought her way through the heavy door carrying an armful of files & papers.

Adam leapt up towards her asking if he could help, and taking the weight of the door with his hand.

The poor woman shrieked and threw her arms in the air, sending the files and papers fluttering to the ground, as she grabbed her face and turned to see Adam standing there, smiling pleasantly.

"What are you doing in here?" She asked, a little un-composed. "I've been waiting some minutes now" he replied pleasantly. "I had an appointment with Mr Tek's head of design, but he seems to be off-site". I have my colleague Dr Wednesday Week with me, although you just missed her as she left for the rest room".

As he'd spoken, the Assistant had been casting a eye around the office. Nothing looked out of place or touched and the large indent in the sofa cushions correlated with the man's story. "I'm very sorry" she stammered, "I wasn't advised of any meetings. I'm afraid you've had a wasted journey. Neither Mr Tek nor his design team are on site, and haven't been for several days".

"You don't know where they are do you?" Asked Adam politely. "It would really be most helpful to our own climate studies if we could just speak with one of them, if only for a few minutes".

"I'm very sorry but I don't know where they've gone" she replied a little huffily. "Mr Tek is his own boss and very often leaves without telling me where he's going or when he'll be back". The last was said with a disdain that for all her professionalism, she thought Tek a rude and arrogant man.

"It wasn't a wasted journey" replied Adam easily, "we had other colleagues in the scientific community, here in America, to visit. Well perhaps some others time when either is available", and turning to exit via the still open door, steered the assistant around by placing an arm around her shoulder.

Wednesday who had been peeking through the tiniest of gaps in the cushions, took the opportunity to leap towards the restroom door, pulling it forward and letting it close back on itself loudly.

Both Adam and the bewildered assistant turned round, as Wednesday smiled and said "have I missed anything?".

"Only that Mr Tek and his whole design team are out of the country and not expected back. I'm afraid we missed them. I was explaining to Mr Tek's charming personal assistant here that the journey is not completely wasted as we have other colleagues in the States we are keen to catch up with".

"If you'll both follow me" said the assistant, "I'll show you to the foyer". Adam extended his arm outwards, indicating she should lead the way, as Wednesday quickly joined him and walked beside him in silence, before they were shown out.

Adam waited until they had cleared the first corner of the building before Wednesday took a sharp inhale and said "That was close". "Yes" replied Adam. "Did you notice that she didn't know when they were due back?".

They were already back at the car by now, as Adam opened the doors, so a familiar voice sounded from the rear space of the car behind the two front seats. "I think you win gold for sofa diving Wednesday". They heard Mate's voice chuckling and then that familiar static noise as Mate lost cohesion and was lost to the four winds.

276

Chapter 24

24. The H15 Chip.

Adam didn't waste a moment, the minute they were on the main road and out of sight of the security gate, in instructing AMIe to convert to flight mode and the i8 climbed steeply up into the crisp blue Autumn sky.

So powerful was their ascent, that Wednesday was pressed back firmly in her seat, as the digital altimeter showed them climbing past 5,000ft already. Still they maintained their steep arcing climb as Adam monitored their course, the car's fuel elements and other systems.

Wednesday managed to turn her head in the building G-Forces, to look out of the window. The ground below as now mere squares of coloured ground, like a patchwork, individual buildings indistinguishable from one another, and only the largest roads showing as thin lines, that seemed to writhe, snake-like, as the traffic moved along.

Now they were levelling off and thankfully the extreme forces she'd experienced during the take-off subsided, and once again the car's interior became a comfortable environment.

"Sorry about the hurried take-off" apologised Adam. "I wanted to get back to the UK as quickly as possible and take a better look at those diagrams".

"What did you see that worried you so much, or rather what did you think you saw, that troubled you?"

"It was the configuration of the two parts of the schematic, when bought together. There's some components in there that you won't find at your local Radio Spares shop. In fact they're highly classified and guarded tighter than Fort Knox. AMIe has several built into her systems". The last Adam said with a half smile.

"And these components have a particular use?" Asked Wednesday.

"Yes. They're more usually found in military communication satellites. In particular, those satellites that confirm presidential location and launch codes for nuclear arsenals. If someone is messing with those, then there aren't many conclusions you can arrive at, and none that end happily ever after".

Biting his lip, Adam asked AMIe to ring a particular number, voice only. After a single ring, the call was answered and young female voice said pleasantly "Drum Accountancy, how may I help?". "May I speak to someone in your export department?" Replied Adam. There was a click as if the call was being put through and then a metallic, computerised voice spoke "checking voice print… voice print confirmed… connecting you now", as Wednesday looked at Adam in wonder, so a familiar voice came on the line "Dr Price and Dr Week? How delightful to hear from you again and so soon after our last meeting. How may I be of service?".

Although the call was voice only, you could almost see the face of the old gentleman smiling like that of a patient parent with a troublesome small child.

"I need to meet with you urgently" began Adam, "Tek's up to something much more sinister than altering global warming data. I've just seen some schematics and blueprints that show he's got his own supply of, or access to, our H15 chips".

"Did you say H for Hotel, 1-5 chips?" Replied a shocked voice.

"Confirmed" said Adam. "Look I need to study these schematics in detail to see the full picture. Can you meet me at the Castle?"

"We're leaving now" replied the old man, "but I do hope this isn't some false alarm. You know how I abhor long journeys".

"I don't think it will be a wasted journey Sir. In fact, it could be the most important journey you've ever taken".

The line went dead and Adam enquired of AMIe their arrival time at Cairn Castle. "Two hours at maximum speed" she replied steadily. "Lets see if we can beat that time" replied Adam. "Over-ride the safety's and go to 110% on the power regulators".

Despite the cars great speed, it managed to give another distinct lurch forward as AMIe engaged the extra power, and the clouds sped up to almost a blur. No vapour trail was left to suggest that anything was in the sky, save for the occasional light blue twinkle caught in the sunlight.

AMIe reported that the front of the car was beginning to over-heat, the dynamic pressures forcing the air out of the way as the car sliced through the thin atmosphere. "We can't hold this speed much longer, at these altitudes" she added pointedly.

Adam took the idea immediately. "AMIe, change our course. Take us into Space and project a course to bring us down as near to the Castle as possible".

"Calculating" replied AMIe. "Course laid in and ready".

"Initiate" shouted Adam, as the car took a more vertical course, pointing straight up towards the blackness of the the approaching void of Space.

As the last blue of Earth's fragile atmosphere was left behind and the car's cockpit became engulfed in that dark, rich blackness, that only a handful of Astronauts have been privileged to experience before, so the car quickly levelled up and almost immediately, began a slow sweeping arc downwards.

"An orbital course will take minutes instead of hours" explained Adam, kicking himself for not thinking of it earlier.

"Re-entry vector coming up" said AMIe, the same message appearing on the car's main screen, which had swapped from typical Airplane instrumentation to the more 3D axis representation of Space navigation.

Wednesday looked out of her window to see the Earth was already rushing upwards to greet them, as the i8 entered the atmosphere in a beautifully crafted dive so as not to create any fireball, normally associated with space craft returning to Earth.

Slipping through the outer-reaches of the atmosphere, the windows outside showing a faint blueness that gathered in density, far below as a thick layer of grey cloud. "Welcome to Scotland" smiled Adam, as the car reverted to normal flight controls, and began braking for the final stages of descent and landing.

Although the car was travelling at speeds many times greater than a normal airplane speed, the rain was lashing the windows of the car, quickly clearing from the windscreen. Suddenly they were through the cloud and the familiar Scottish landscape of Loch Earn was directly ahead of them.

Adam was bringing the i8 in low, in the neighbouring, uninhabited valley, to shield their approach from the villagers and visitors to Loch Earn, before taking a sweeping turn at the bottom and approaching the Castle cave entrance they'd left from, only yesterday.

The car seemed to come to a virtual, hovering halt, just before the cave entrance, as it slid apart to allow the car access. Adam guided the car forward, spinning it 180 degrees as he did so, before setting down with the merest bump, which confirmed they were finally back on land. Already the cave entrance had closed up, and lights had now come on automatically in the hangar like garage.

Heather was standing a little way back, waiting to greet them. Her enquiring look showed that she was surprised to see them back so quickly.

As they climbed out of the car, Wednesday's legs a little wobbly after their hurried journey through Space, so Heather ran to hug her, and asked Adam how the mission had gone?

"We've got lots to tell you" replied Adam grimly. "Wednesday, why don't you go with Heather and get a drink and something to eat while I take our findings down to the main lab. I'll see you there shortly", and with that he turned and was gone.

"What's happened?" Asked Heather.

"I need a stiff drink" replied Wednesday weakly, "and I'll tell you all".

Over a generous measure of brandy, Wednesday told Heather how they'd got into Tek's offices with the help of Mate, before discovering the schematics and drawings, split into two separate drawings for secrecy, before Adam had put two and two together and insisted they leave immediately.

She then lightened the mood by recounting how she'd dived for the space behind the sofa when the office door had opened, and Tek's unsuspecting PA had entered the room, and Adam's sweet talking them out of the tricky situation.

She finished by telling Heather about the in-flight phone call with the old gentleman, and the disclosure of the H15 chips being used in the circuit. Electronic chips that are normally under lock & key.

At the mention of the H15, Heather gasped. "Am I the only one who hasn't heard of this H15 chip?" Asked Wednesday, slightly exasperated.

"I'd only heard of it through a journalistic contact". "It was mentioned in connection with a story about discrepancies in the Ministry records at one of their most secure, top-secret, locations, but that was a couple of years ago now".

"And do you know why they're so heavily guarded?" Asked Wednesday.

"No, we could never get a source on the story to corroborate it. Of course there's the usual 'grassy-knoll gang' rumours that its to do with decoding alien radio signals or launching nuclear weapons or something like that. You know conspiracy theorists".

"Well, Adam discovered these H15 chips had been used in Tek's satellites and immediately instructed us to leave and come back here. He even rang that old gent on the journey and asked him to get here as quickly as possible" explained Wednesday.

"C'mon, I think I feel well enough to join Adam in the Lab".

The two of them walked through the castle and passed quickly through the double air-lock system to the laboratory area.

As they came into the main room, still chatting, they found Adam staring at a large 3D floating display of the circuit board that had hastened their journey home.

Various circuit lines were lighting up to simulate power or signals passing along them, as the blue dot representing the signal, went from component to component in a beautiful, almost orchestrated fashion.

"Freeze there AMIe" said Adam, as the two approached. A smile now replacing the earlier worried frown he'd worn.

"Found something?" Asked Heather.

"Yes, as a matter of fact I have". He was about to continue when AMIe announced there were visitors at the door of the Castle. The camera showed an old gentleman, accompanied by two heavier, younger men and a more academic looking figure behind the three.

Adam quickly went up to the hallway and opened the door to greet his guests, who came in quickly, the old gent walking to stand back to the roaring log fire, and rubbing his hands together behind his back.

"Your call implied a level of seriousness, hence my colleague from the electronic science division has joined us Dr Price. So what can you tell us?".

"I can do more than that Sir, I can show you, if you'll follow me through to my workshop. This way if you please".

Adam guided the 2 men through the airlocks, the two security men remained in the hallway, glad of the chance to enjoy the warming fire unobserved.

As they entered the main laboratory area, so Adam pointed to Heather and Wednesday and said "I think you're acquainted with Miss Lightly and Dr Week?". The old gent stepped forward and shook both their hands saying he was delighted to meet them both again, whilst also introducing his colleague from their science division, who merely nodded at the introduction, but made no move to also shake their hands or reveal his name.

From his shoulder bag, he removed a small laptop, but Adam stopped him before he'd had chance to open it. "I don't think you'll need that" he explained helpfully, continuing "besides, I don't allow any outside devices to connect to my systems here.. for security reasons you understand?".

The man merely nodded and placed the un-opened laptop back in its protective bag.

"Please take a seat everyone" said Adam, pointing to the various stools and chairs around the main central projection table.

"We discovered a number of blueprints and schematic drawings at Tek's Vandenberg offices, and found these two files that at first, looked like any other circuit layout, BUT, when these two particular files were bought together and overlapped" the 3D projection shifted to show the two drawings coming together as one, "you'll see the H15 chips is revealed as one of several new components.

At first, I wasn't fully sure of their function within this particular circuit, but having returned here to my workshop and with the help of the projection screens, I've been able to trace back the exact function these circuits were designed for".

Adam pointed to several blue dots that were travelling across the network of circuitry, before converging on a single processor, judging by its rating, of considerable power and computational skill.

Adam continued "you see here where the circuits converge into this processor, a quite remarkable bit of design I might add, runs on virtually no power and does away with the usual cooling requirements of normal processors, where the true purpose of the programming is revealed.

I've managed to hack into that code and this is what I found".

A new diagram appeared, showing a signal being transmitted simultaneously from 15 transmitters in orbit around the Earth.

A simulation then showed these signals being received at military listening and communication centres, like the Cheltenham GCHQ building. The signals were relayed to various command posts, that most worryingly were all attached to nuclear missile sites in the UK, North America and Soviet Union.

"I believe, that Tek is planning on using his global temperature monitoring satellites to in fact start World War 3, with a nuclear war between the East and the West. Somehow, he's going to simulate presidential orders to fire those weapons.

As you know, the safety protocols for launching Nuclear weapons are complex and include the system confirming the present location of the President as well as that 12-hour window of launch codes.

I'm assuming the Russians have a similar system in place", to which the old man nodded.

Adam placed his hands flat on the table, as the projection fell away. "I don't think Tek is planning an all-out annihilation of the Earth, but merely a way to take out the two major world powers or perhaps hold them to ransom. His choice of the North Pole is clever as its the area predicted to suffer the least amount of radioactivity following any nuclear confrontation".

"But what does he hope to gain from such a war?" Asked Wednesday. "Surely nothing can be worth that kind of risk?"

"And want about reprisals" asked Heather. "He wouldn't hope to get away without incurring the wrath of one or more countries?"

"I think" said Adam, trying to choose his words carefully, "Tek isn't interested in extortion or reprisals. If you look at the map of strategic launch sites he's hoping to control, and their respective targets in Russia, he's hoping to take out the World governments and seats of power in one fell swoop.

Yes there'll be some local anarchy and civil disorder but effectively, it will leave the World open to being conquered by any organisation large enough to march in and claim that land, resource or population.

You've seen the barracks all set up on the Ice field outside his mountain HQ. Enough to house a small army wouldn't you say? And the means and the technology to insert relatively small numbers of well trained troops, into any territory and take control with minimal offensive action".

"He's completely insane of course" finished Adam.

"So how do we stop him?" Asked the old gent, with a smile that suggested he already had a pretty good idea of what Adam was going to suggest next.

"Alert your counterparts in the USA and Russia. Tell them to be on their guard for an encrypted attack on their launch systems. When it comes, they'll have minutes to respond before the fail-safes kick in and the launches can't be over-ridden.

I'm going to work on something here and make a direct attempt to stop Tek myself".

290

Price: Polestarr

"You're going to stop him?" Asked the old gent.

"Yes, I'm the only one that can" replied Adam so earnestly that both Wednesday and Heather found themselves nodding in agreement.

The old gent took his leave, escorted back to the entrance hall by Heather, whilst Adam and Wednesday began working on Adam's scheme.

Adam had been particularly vague about what exactly he intended to do and it was only when Heather re-joined them in the laboratory, that he expanded on his plan.

Before he could start however, Heather interrupted him with an update on her own investigations whilst they'd flown to Vandenberg.

"It seems you were right about Tek having more than just a casual involvement in other companies" she began. "His name cropped up, buried amongst a long list of investors in several start-up electronics companies; all fronts of course.

Several useless patents filed, but it was only when I stepped back, that a pattern emerged. They were all using some form of encoded transmitter technology. That fits with your idea of Tek hacking the most secure systems on the planet".

"There's more" she continued, "and it may be nothing, but my friend at the paper had heard of one of the companies mentioned somewhere else and did a little more digging. It seems one of them was developing some sort of anti-sonar jamming buoys and had requested the help of the American Navy in deploying the buoys."

"Why a naval ship?" Asked Wednesday. "Surely any oceanic research vessel would be capable of dropping these buoys off at designated co-ordinates and monitoring them".

"You're right of course" said Adam, not looking up from the computer screen he was sat at. "Heather, did your contact say what specific vessel the company had asked for?"

"Why yes. It was the USS Apollo".

"The Apollo" mused Adam, continuing to tap on the keyboard in front of him. AMIe had been monitoring the conversation of course, and interrupted with "Excuse me, but the USS Apollo is the first Nuclear Submarine with a stealth coating technology".

"Stealth coating?" Queried Wednesday.

"Yes, not your average submarine, and still undergoing trials at sea. The hull has a particular
292

construction that makes it invisible to normal radar and sonar. If it runs silent, its undetectable, which would make sense if you're deploying these anti-sonar devices".

"What did the US Navy say? Did they agree?"

"There's nothing to suggest they even replied" said Heather. "No correspondence by return, and no forwarding of the request to the relevant departments within the military for further consideration".

"It's a curiosity that of all the armed forces, the Navy has always been more amenable to requests for assistance from private organisations. From Jungle expeditions to exploring the Poles. Could Tek be gambling on their assistance?"

"Tek doesn't gamble" retorted Adam. "Every decision, every action is planned minutely and at least seven steps ahead of everyone else. Every eventuality has been played out, meaning its almost impossible to surprise the man".

"Almost impossible?" Asked Wednesday.

"Well when I say he's seven steps ahead of everyone, that's everyone except me. Now I know what he's up to, I'm eight steps ahead of the game".

Jonathan C. Crouch

Chapter 25

25. Tek's Tokyo Rose.

The table was being cleared by servants who earlier, had served the lavish meal to Tek and his guests. All business partners who'd paid substantial sums to him in return for being able to sit out the oncoming nuclear onslaught, in the safety of Tek's polar fortress.

As they'd moved away to sit in the comfortably fitted out lounge area, brandy's in hand, one of them, a tall thin man, no more than 35 years of age, had sidled up alongside Tek and whispered "how long to go?"

Tek had only smiled and tapped a finger to the side of his nose, and the person who had asked the question was left feeling like a small child who's been excluded from the neighbourhood gang.

Some of the others had watched him approach Tek and smiled at the thought that they'd been right not to ask the one question, everyone was burning to ask.

Now they were seated, the doors closed silently shutting the room off from everyone else, the lights dimmed and a holographic projector lowered from the ceiling and so began the briefing as a 3D holographic figure of an attractive young woman, walked around a slowly spinning globe, pointing out specific places, that then lit with a red spot on the map.

The audience watched silently, whilst Tek studied their faces intently. He had no need to listen to the presentation - he'd recorded it, using computer synthesis to alter the voice to that of the women who continued to walk around the globe, pointing and raising her arms to emphasise a particular point, while the Earth continued its slow & deliberate rotation.

A modern day Tokyo Rose, thought Tek.

The presentation was coming to an end and Tek was relieved to see that throughout, the men's faces had remained impassive, if not a little excited, at the prospect of the oncoming storm, that would see each of them installed as Governors of a new world order, after the immediate radioactive dust had settled.

The presentation ended with the globe highlighting countries, grouped in various colours, that denoted the total area each Governor would be in charge of.

Price: Polestarr

The America's Tek had reserved for himself.

The presentation had answered one vital question. How long they were expected to stay at the North Pole, before it was safe to leave.

Tek himself joined the conversation as the holographic figure shimmered and melted away, leaving only the globe still spinning lazily in front of the men.

"Today's nuclear weapons are much more sophisticated than the first devices dropped on Japan by the Americans. They can now be programmed to deliver an exact destructive yield that is incredibly focused.

It will be possible to destroy the targets with minimal blast diameters of less than a quarter mile. The World is no good to us if the infrastructures of power, water and industry are damaged.

Once the initial launch is over, we'll be able to instruct conventional weapons systems to fire on themselves. The Navy for example, sinking their own fleets, whilst Air Forces shoot their own planes from the skies.

And with no communications, land forces will be impotent, fragmented and completely alone.

And now if you'll excuse me gentleman, I have lots to over-see, before tomorrow. Please stay and finish your drinks".

Tek rose as he spoke, and walked out of the room quickly. Once through the door, he operated the closing mechanism, whilst similar, heavier doors, shut silently, sealing the room off.

Moving to a smaller office, still larger than your average board room, he sat at the large desk and pressed his thumb to a small area on the smoked glass top.

Instantly the desk top came alive, like a giant screen, showing the lounge area and the men sitting about talking amongst themselves. A small rectangular icon was flashing slowly, the word 'Initiate' in faint red lettering.

Tek's hand paused momentarily over the icon, before pressing it with his index finger.

The icon turned to green, but continued flashing whilst a small digital display counted down from ten.

In the room, the holographic globe had stopped spinning as it depicted digits counting down from ten. The men all stopped, fascinated by the counting digits, accompanied by the same soft female voice of the presenter.

As it reached zero, so the presenters voice changed to a maniac laugh in Tek's own voice, followed by a barely audible whine that quickly rose in pitch as to become ear-piercing. The men all dropped to their knees, clutching their heads, hands clasped over ears.

The whine continued to rise until it was silent, producing the merest vibration as one by one, the heavy brandy glasses the men had been holding moments earlier, began shattering with small popping sounds as they exploded. Still the men held the heads in agony, their faces contorted in pain, eyes squeezed shut, as a new popping sound could be heard, and one by one, their heads exploded in a red mist.

Tek had remained unmoved during the whole scene, and now he quietly moved to switch off the screens, one by one, before turning around in the large chair, as fingers pursed together, he studied the ice-field outside, cold, barren, unyielding, but of infinite majesty and grandeur.

***

Adam had continued working long into the night, and when Wednesday and Heather emerged from their rooms the following morning, they found him laying under the i8 besides a second car that seemed to have emerged out of Scottish mist.

On hearing their footsteps approaching, he waved a foot at them as he said "help yourself to coffee - there's a fresh pot keeping warm on the far workbench".

"Have you been down here all night?" Asked Heather.

"Afraid so" replied Adam. "I had a lot to get ready".

"No sign of Mate?" "None" replied Wednesday. "We were getting quite worried about him. He's been gone even longer than usual".

"Where did the new car come from?" Asked Wednesday.

"It's an old Mk1 I had in the basement" laughed Adam. "Seriously though, I had AMIe fly it here last night from one of my 'garages'. It's got a very important mission to go on".

"How did AMIe fly the car?" Asked Heather, incredulous.

"This one has full remote control abilities. An upgrade I've been meaning to retro-fit to the newer model, when I get a moment, but there wasn't time for the fabrication of the components and test flights for trim, so I bought in reinforcements.".

Price: Polestarr

The new car was a dull metallic grey colour, with fully blacked out windows. With none of the tell-tale blue neon edges or detailing, it looked positively menacing like some brooding bird of prey.

"So" said Heather, hitching herself up onto a high stool next to the work bench, where the coffee was bubbling away, "what's the plan? You do have a plan don't you?"

Adam extracted himself from under the car, sitting up and wiping his hands on a clean rag. Picking up the small collection of tools he'd been working with, he walked over to Heather and turned around to lean against the edge of the bench, scattering the handful of tools into a large plastic tray.

"I do have a 'plan' as you put in" he smiled. "And it's going to need all our efforts. I wish Mate was here to help but we'll have to proceed as though he isn't and hope he's able to materialise in time. Follow me".

The three walked back to the laboratory with the large 3D imaging display as Adam started tapping on a keyboard, and AMIe initiated the projection.

"Our attack comes in 3 parts. Firstly, we need to disrupt Tek's satellites and break their unified collection. Wednesday, you'll be here with AMIe to help you, disrupting the program via a hack into Tek's control room operations.

The second part is a little trickier. AMIe is going to remote pilot the spare i8 and take it into orbit and destroy one of Tek's satellites. I suspect the satellites have their own armoury installed as well as evasive movements programmed for just such an eventuality. I don't think Tek is a man to leave anything to chance.

The third and final part is for me. Taking the other car, I'm going to fly up to the Artic and confront Tek and his organisation myself. I'm hoping I can do enough to stop his plans to take over the World's nuclear and conventional arsenals".

Heather was about to ask what her role was going to be, when the phone rang and Adam pounced onto it, quickly lifting the receiver to his ear.

".. And you've been able to secure the vessel we discussed?" Asked Adam of the voice on the other end of the call, "that's great news. I'll brief the Captain when I'm on board. Tell them to arrange for my arrival in 45 minutes at the co-ordinates discussed, and thank you Sir".

Adam hung up the call and turned excitedly to Heather & Wednesday, his eyes glinting with excitement. "I've just received confirmation from my friend in Whitehall, that my request for a little additional help has been arranged".

"Heather, how would you like to take a ride in a submarine?"

Chapter 26

26. That Sinking Feeling.

There was much to complete before Adam and Heather could depart. Adam was showing Wednesday how to initiate the hacks and programs he and AMIe had been working on earlier, to get access to and stop Tek's computerised terror plans.

Heather had changed into one of the comfortable black 'action suits' and jokingly remarked that she looked like something out of a super-hero film. "The suit has built-in comfort against weather extremes and would even save you if you were exposed to the Artic Sea. Thankfully, Submarines are a lot more comfortable now, but the suit will mean you're prepared for anything" replied Adam.

Adam himself was also changed into a similar suit, with various straps and pouches about his person, containing a number of intriguing bits of electronics and surveillance devices.

It was time to launch the remote control i8 and Adam sat at AMIe's main console and initiated the remote take off protocol. As the cave doorway slid back, so the i8 rose and quickly exited the entrance, which closed almost immediately.

Wishing Wednesday good luck, Adam and Heather took their seats in the other car, as Adam closed the doors, and initiated the vertical take-off as AMIe opened the cave entrance once again and Adam and Heather took to the skies above the Highlands of Scotland.

Adam hadn't explained to Wednesday exactly how she was supposed to get onto the Submarine. A question she asked him now.

"The Apollo is going to surface and I'm going to hover and lower you down to their deck. Simple!".

"It doesn't sound simple" replied Heather worriedly. "What about the wind that'll be swinging me about in the air. How will they hope to catch me, without me taking a swim?"

"Don't worry" smiled Adam. "The crew is well trained in aerial transfers. Just hold tight and you'll be on board in a flash. We'll be able to talk during the descent and capture. It will be fine".

Secretly though, Adam was a little apprehensive at the approaching transfer to the submarine. Although extremely well trained, including having rescue divers and a small dinghy ready in case of emergency, aerial transfers were not without their risks, especially if the weather was bad. The weather was steadily worsening as they flew over the sea towards their rendezvous point with the USS Apollo.

Below the waves, gliding serenely and untroubled by the turbulent waters above, the USS Apollo was holding a small circular course at the co-ordinates they'd been given. At the appointed time, the Captain raised the periscope, took a last 360 degree look around on the surfaces before retracting the periscope and giving the quiet command to surface.

Adam and Heather were studying the waves below when suddenly, a monstrous black coning tower broke the surface of the frothing waves, as slowly, the body of the submarine became visible, waves whipping over the main deck as the Submarine pitched in the heavy waves.

Adam and Heather were now both wearing headsets as the ear-pieces crackled and a calm voice instructed them to get ready.

Below on the deck, there were already sailors in heavy water survival suits, manning the main deck, flat and slippery looking, fixing hand rails and lines fore and aft. In the more protected cockpit of the coming tower, men were making ready with a large telescopic pole that ended in a large hoop, which could be used to capture and tighten on a persons leg or arm.

The radioman's voice told them to take final position for lowering and Adam gently nudged the car sideways until it was directly over the coning tower. The sailors looked up at the underbelly of the i8, marvelling at the engineering and sure-handedness of the incredible machine's flight control.

Now Adam opened Heather's door and with a quick 'Good luck", the car seat moved out sideways and a winch built into the seat's headrest, & attached to a harness Heather was wearing for the descent, began lowering her down gracefully.

Although the strong winds continued to batter Heather, causing her to spin slowly, the specially designed winch with its dual cables, was doing a remarkable job of holding her steady, as sea spray whipped about her face, so the safety of the submarine approached.

A sailor was already brandishing the catchment pole in front of him, trying to lasso her foot. Once, twice he missed as the wind and boats movements combined to make him swipe and miss, but on the third attempt he was successful, catching her foot expertly and drawing the noose tight, to bring her to safety.

Many hands caught her harness and limbs as she was lowered to the coning towers deck. A sailor unclipped her harness and Adam wound the mechanism and seat back into the car. Closing the door, he circled the submarine twice waving to Heather, who despite the cold was grinning like a Cheshire Cat. With a final wave from her, he peeled away and headed for Tek's base on the Artic ice.

Heather followed one of the sailors that had caught her, down the narrow ladder, through layers off steel and pipes, until they dropped into a larger control room. The other sailors who had also been on the tower, followed and the final one had shut and screwed tight the water-tight hatches.

Stifling a sudden claustrophobic fear to run for the open hatch, she shivered as the final metallic clang sounded and they were sealed in.

A sailor bearing the insignia of a First Officer came forward and welcomed her aboard. "I'll take you to the Captain now" he'd merely stated, before turning to another sailor of rank and ordering them to dive.

There were no klaxons, shouts of Dive Dive Dive, or in fact anything to show they were being ordered to submerge. The same officer who'd been instructed to dive merely picked up a microphone from an

309

overhead radio set and said quietly "we're preparing to dive".

The First Officer noticed her bemused look and said "It's not like the films is it?". "No" she replied, thankful for the conversation to take her mind off of the thought of being trapped in a steel box below the waves.

"How quickly can we submerge?" She asked. "Well as we have guests aboard and plenty of open sea ahead of us, we're taking a nice slow descent trajectory. We can drop like a stone if we need to".

They moved forward leaving the calm atmosphere of the control room behind, Heather noticed the two helmsman's seats were fitted with the kinds of harnesses usually seen in fighter jet cockpits.

Down a panelled corridor to a small door, which simply said Captain on it. The First Office knocked once and a voice answered come in. He opened the door and showed Heather through, closing the door behind her.

Wednesday was monitoring the remote control flight of the second car as it reached the upper limits of Earth's atmosphere and entered Space itself. Everything had gone to plan so far, and Adam had radioed her to let them know that Heather was safely on board the USS Apollo.

Adam asked her how she was getting on with the process of gaining access to Tek's systems which connected and controlled the information and signal stream. Admittedly, Adam had given her a mammoth task but with AMIe's help, and Adam's earlier programming template to follow, she had gained access to the first satellite.

Adam was still travelling over the sea bearing down on the ice field where Tek had his base, when the emergency suit he had stowed for Mate, was ejected from the compartment in the dashboard it was stored in, to unroll on the passenger seat. Adam had barely time to turn and face the suite before it unfurled completely and began filling out as Mate resumed his cohesive form.

As the last fingertip expanded and filled, so the indicator lights on the collar lit and Mate spoke. "Where are we?"

Adam filled him on their plan and explained that he and now Mate were headed for Tek's ice mountain fortress. "I know you didn't fare to well in the temperatures last time" explained Adam, "which is why I've added a small heating solution to the suits environment. Hopefully, it will stave off the worst effects of the cold, but its purely hypothetical, since we have no real data on the effects of cold on your form or abilities".

"I've noticed that my periods of re-construction are more intermittent - erratic and shorter" replied Mate. "Do you think it's a temporary thing or is this permanent"?

"I really don't know" answered Adam truthfully, "but once we get through this, I intend to devote all my time to finding out my friend".

Mate only nodded in reply. Already out of the windscreen, the first frozen ice floes were beginning to appear in the grey waters below, with the first ice-shelf mass approaching in the distance.

On board the Submarine, Heather was finishing her briefing to the Captain.. "so as you can see Captain Williams, whilst we're taking out the Satellites and software, Dr Price is attempting to infiltrate Tek's polar HQ and confront the man in person. There may be fail-safes or other codes, perhaps bio-metric ones, coded only to Tek himself". It was the last part that Adam had admitted to the others, was the most worrying and why he had to be confronted in person, rather than dealt with by force.

Price: Polestarr

"And I'm to land the team of Marines on the ice to assist Dr Price is that it?" Queried the Captain, pursing his lips in quite contemplation of what that would entail from his men and his ship.

"Correct" replied Heather, adding "and I'll be going with them".

Williams reached behind his chair to a wall mounted radio and picked up the handset. Clicking the 'talk' button, he enquired of the bridge what their ETA was to the coordinates of the ice-field they were to attempt to land on.

"We're in position now Captain" came the assured voice.

"Very well, myself and Miss Lightly will join you in the control room shortly. Maintain our position and silent running please". Turning to Heather, he said "perhaps you'd care to join me for a little torpedo training?".

"I'd be fascinated" replied Heather, returning his smile, as she rose and they left the Office.

Adam was bringing the car in low and under cover of the huge ice mountain, hoping that it afforded them some stealth of approach. The i8 was already in a cloaked mode, making it virtually invisible to radar and human sight, but Adam was taking no chances.

As they neared the chosen touchdown site, a small plateau behind a screening ridge of icy hummocks, dune like in their smoothness from the continuing blowing snow and ice particles, so Adam spoke with Wednesday and Heather simultaneously.

"You'll be pleased to hear that Mate has rejoined me, and will assist with the final entrance to Tek's HQ. Timing is going to be critical. At the first sign of any trouble, Tek could launch his destructive plans. We've got to be absolutely sure we have everything in place before we strike.

Wednesday, how's the satellite and communications access coming?"

"All ready" replied Wednesday nervously. "The execute button is flashing on my desktop ready to initiate".

"Great and what of the second i8 AMIe"?

"That's holding position just off the port of Satellite Alpha, weapons armed ready to target".

"Heather here". "The Captain's a little worried that the first torpedo strike might not make a hole big enough for the whole ship to fit through. Of course once we fire the first torpedo, they will know we're here".

"Understood" replied Adam. "It's probably best if Mate and I effect entry alone, whilst Wednesday and AMIe deal with their tasks simultaneously, with you and the Marines, following on in a second wave to close down the ice-fortress".

"AMIe, give everyone a synchronised 10 minute countdown on my mark. Mark!" And Adam manoeuvred the i8 and bought it to a vertical landing on the ice.

Once down, Adam grabbed his thermal outer garments and goggles, fitting them snugly in place before exiting the car. Mate had already dissipated from the suit and was waiting patiently at the doorway - the same one through which Adam had entered and rescued him before.

Adam shortly joined him, having had to duck down and hide from one of Tek's regular patrols, the 4 men in their bright orange suits, trudging along in classic single file, roped together at 3 metre intervals, lest one of them should fall through a crevasse.

Checking the dial of his watch, he motioned with 5 fingers the last 5 seconds of the countdown, before reaching for the door's handle.

In Space, the i8 that had been floating lazily came to life as displays lit up and manoeuvring thrusters fired bringing it into line with the unsuspecting satellite, just ahead.

A last weapons and guidance check and the i8 let off a single rocket projectile, that homed in on the target. It struck exactly in the mid-rift of the satellites main body, showering floating debris out into the vacuum of space, as the satellite began rotating from the blasts impact. Small electrical fires burned briefly before being extinguished by Space itself.

In Scotland, Wednesday saw the explosion take place on the monitor, and watched as the i8 turned and headed for home, its task complete. She'd already hit the 'enable' button on her screen to coincide with the rockets detonation, and leant back, apparently satisfied, as the streams of data flying past on the screens in front of her, confirmed the disabling hack was working and Tek's ability to remotely launch the missiles was being removed.

In the Artic fortress that was Tek's base, alarms started sounding as engineers and programmers registered the loss of the satellite and the closing and eradication of the launch program.

Tek strode into the control room, and lifted the controller by his lapels up out of his seat and inches above the ground. "What's happening?" He growled, as the controller, gasped and struggled to free himself from Tek's grip. Tek dropped him into his chair as he spun him around to face the bank of monitors and the faces of the controllers in the trenches below.

"Every systems gone haywire. We've lost a satellite - it's been totally destroyed" he said disbelievingly, "and the launch programs are erasing themselves. I'm afraid to report that we have lost all ability to launch or take control of any weapons, of any kind".

"Having problems Tek?"

Tek spun round to see Adam standing in front of him, framed by the doorway built into the gallery wall that ran behind the control room.

"You" growled Tek, reaching out for Adam's neck. "But how?

"Once I'd discovered what you were really up to, I took out your satellite and communications ability. It's over Tek! Surrender and come with me now".

"Over" croaked Tek, "it's barely started Dr Price. I'm afraid you've under-rated my abilities, my strategy, my brilliance. Did you really think it would be so easy to disable a plan I've spent years perfecting?" He touched the side of his wrist watch, and spoke the word "initiate", before Adam could reach his arm and stop him.

Instantly, monitors that had been shouting meltdown now came on in crystal clarity, as one by one processes started and an external camera angle from one of the satellites in Space, showed the top dish section detaching and moving away from the body. Even the one destroyed by Adam's remote i8 had detached the undamaged saucer dish section as it to moved to a new position.

In Scotland, Wednesday's jubilation had turned to horror as she watched new programs start running and despite her's and AMIe's best efforts they were completely locked out.

Heather nodded to the Captain. It was time, Quietly, the order to 'Fire' was given as the Exec tracked the progress and detonation of the first torpedo. The ship shuddered as the weapon detonated and the Captain quickly lifted the periscope to take a look at the damage they'd inflicted on the ice's surface from below.

A small crack had appeared; the weak artic sunlight barely registering through the gap, which was already closing up and freezing over.

"Launch Two" instructed the Captain calmly, and again the same shudder was felt through the ship on detonation.

Price: Polestarr

Taking another peek, it was clear that a much larger hole had been opened in the ice above. Large enough for the coning tower to fit through anyway, as the submarine manoeuvred into perfect position below the newly made opening, and blew ballast to rise upwards quickly, splintering the ice in large flat shards that fell either side of the steel tower, as the submarine made surface on the ice-field directly in front of Tek's mountain HQ.

Marines quickly deployed from the towers hatches, as orange suited figures rushed from the mountain cave entrance and began firing at the invaders.

As more Marines joined the fight, assembling larger automatic guns, which they pivoted and turned on Tek's forces, so Tek's men fell back into the relative shelter and safety of the fortress.

Meanwhile, in Tek's control room, he and Adam continued to square off against each other. "In ten minutes Dr Price, my satellites will have re-positioned themselves and a smaller more portable computer system will initiate the final destructive missile launch. There is nothing you can do to stop that now. Not even you".

"I'm sure I'll think of something"replied Adam with false bravado for although his mind was working quickly, he hadn't been able to come up with a

319

resolution to the problems he faced, as Tek produced a hand gun and pointing it at Adam's chest, and ordered his men to remove Adam to where he might be more comfortable.

Chapter 27

27. Battle Under The Ice.

Outside the battle on the ice raged as both sides re-thought their strategy and positions.

With the regular crew of the submarine pinned down inside for their own safety, Heather could only wonder how Adam was getting on inside.

As it turned out, Adam was not going anywhere. He'd been beaten by Tek's men before being roughly thrown into a small cell, its walls made of thick, hard ice. Only the door was metal, equally think and unyielding with no visible hinges on Adam's side or lock mechanism. Only a small, high grill, could be opened from the outside.

The temperature was well below freezing and despite his artic action suit, ripped in places from the beating he's endured, without the thermal outer layers he had been wearing, the cold was numbing, sapping both bodily energy and cognitive ability.

He heard a slight scuffling noise outside, like a rodent scampering with claws on ice, when the door swung open and the faint tinged outline of a figure hovered in front of him. "Room service" said Mate, as Adam faltered, then stepped with more strength through the open door to greet his friend.

Behind the opened door, a stunned guard lay, a look of horror and amazement on his face, as Mate explained that he'd given the guard quite a nasty shock, semi-appearing in front of him, before knocking him out cold.

"I'm glad to see you" replied Adam. "I thought I was going to freeze to death in there".

"I'm sorry it took me so long to find you" replied Mate, turning his hand to show Adam the torn off collar of his normal suit. "After I'd cannibalised the suit, to be able to roam around unseen, I'd lost track of where Tek had taken you. Speaking of which, Tek's not in the control room anymore, and I can't find him anywhere".

"He won't have gone far" replied Adam, as they continued to make their way along the maze of corridors which Adam was pretty sure led to Tek's control room. "His plan needs this equipment, this set-up and he can't simply abandon the base. He'd have no protection from any possible radioactive fall-out".

Price: Polestarr

They'd moved quickly and were already at the control room entrance. Mate went in first, his invisibility essential to their not being detected, before motioning Adam to follow. The room was empty, seemingly running on auto-pilot, as still active screens showed the satellites continuing to re-align.

Tek's words "a small more portable system" rung in Adam's ears as he sat at one of the larger stations and began the login process.

A series of files came up, and he selected schematics. A drawing of the entire base started unfurling , as lines joined up to form rooms and corridors, the entrance to the ice-field, and more floors below.

Outside, the marines had reached an impasse with the forces inside the hangar, unable to open the main hangar door and take the fight on.

On one of the screens inside, Adam saw the forces gathered at the hangar door, and selecting another system, over-rode the security lock, making the door start to open.

Outside there was a cheer from the Marines, as they quickly took advantage of the surprise on the enemy faces, and stormed the hangar area. The final battle was brief and complete as the Marines took the hangar, before moving off in smaller groups to secure the rest of the base from Tek's men.

Back at the schematic, which continued to unravel and reveal, a lift shaft became discernible, located behind Tek's desk in the private office behind them.

It travelled for a number of feet, far under the ice field before coming to stop at a small loading stage. A docking jetty!

"Of course" exclaimed Adam to Mate. Tek was boasting about his portable back up system.. he must have a submarine down there".

"But I though he'd already asked for the Apollo"? Replied Mate.

"Yes and that was refused - obviously - since we've got her, but what if there was another 'Sub? Perhaps a sister ship with the same stealth capabilities?"

"C'mon, we need to get back to the i8 and warn the others. Heather and the crew of the Apollo may be in grave danger".

"That" replied Mate "and the small matter of saving the World".

Adam ran back through the base, whilst Mate vanished, meeting a team of Marines on the way.

Hardly stopping, he instructed them to get back to the Sub as fast at they could, while he went to contact the Captain, Heather and Wednesday.

Grabbing an outdoor coat and goggles off of a stunned guard, laying near the door, he quickly donned the garments and rushed out onto the ice, towards the car.

As he approached, AMIe opened the doors automatically, and as he seated himself, so Mate re-appeared beside him. Bringing touch-screens to life, Adam contacted Wednesday and Heather simultaneously, and explained the situation. Both women winced when they saw his beaten face, but Adam insisted he was fine and besides there was no time.

"Wednesday. Get AMIe to turn round the remote i8 and head back to that satellite. We need to take another shot at disabling it, and as many of the others as we can. Be warned their likely to have some anti-attack tricks up their proverbial satellite sleeves, we didn't encounter last time.

Heather, I need the Captain to take the Sub down as quickly as possible. I think there's a secret sister ship to the USS Apollo, and Tek's got her tethered up at a secret docking portal reached from his base. It's likely he'll try and escape in it, launch his deadly attack and take you out in the process".

"What about you?" Asked Heather.

"I'm going to try and take Tek's sub head-on with Mate's help. That launch has got to be stopped whatever the cost".

Up in Space, the remotely operated i8 was nearing the position of the closest satellite. As it targeted the small dish array, the device emitted some kind of sonic wave, that blew every electronic system in the car, which began to oscillate madly, like a gyroscope at a disco, as it spun past the satellite and tumbled out into Space.

Wednesday reported the cars loss to Adam, who was by now airborne and circling the submarine, which was hurriedly preparing to submerge.

As the last of the watertight hatches were closed, the antenna lowered, the large steel coning tower slipped beneath the ice, leaving a frozen slushy froth in its wake as the hole it had left tried to re-freeze itself shut.

Not wasting a moment once the sub was clear of the gap it had made and underway beneath the ice, Adam took the car into a steep climb, only to rollover and dive headlong through the slowly shrinking gap.

Flipping the car 90 degrees to enter the ice in perfect alignment with the length of the rapidly narrowing passage, it plunged into the icy sea, and came about to search for Tek's own submarine, lurking somewhere in the depths below.

Adam switched the car's displays to full sonar mode, as the central screen showed the jagged outlines of ice ridges from the surface that fell into the depths. Soon they picked up the lift shaft and docking structure they's seen on the plans of Tek's ice fortress but if there was a submarine, it had long gone.

Adam now noticed that the lift shaft continued down past the docking level. Sinking the car down, level with the structure, Adam tilted the tiny submersible downward to see what lay ahead. It didn't take long. A few more feet and a glow started to emanate from the pea-green depths. Closer they fell until the structure came into view.

It was a massive metal sphere, free of ice and emanating the strange glow. "What do you make of that?" Asked Adam to Mate

"It looks like a reactor of some kind" replied Mate. "Perhaps the source of power for the entire structure above".

Adam whistled. "Its' pumping out some serious energy. Enough to run a small town if need be".

Suddenly the car's sonar pinged wildly and a shrill whistling noise could be heard passing close to the rear of the car. A Torpedo!

Adam took the controls and swung the car around to face whatever had fired at them. Too late, another high pitched whistle told them another torpedo was coming for them. Adam threw the cars controls to the right as the submersible took a spinning dive to starboard and the second torpedo sped off into the distant sea.

Mate was looking wildly about them for a sight of whatever was shooting torpedos at them. Through the gloom, a large round bulk appeared, its cylindrical shape tapering to a flat point, from which two propellers were churning fast.

Despite its size, the large submarine seemed to have no trouble in matching their tiny craft's course and turn of speed.

"It is some sort of sister ship to the USS Apollo" cried Adam, trying to alternate turns to port & starboard in an attempt to escape the chasing submarine.

"Tek must have his own crew on board, & taken over the ship" said Mate as another high pitched sound came over the sonar. This sounded different to the earlier torpedos and seconds later, it stopped completely. Instantly, there was a loud flash as a mine exploded ahead of the car. Adam quickly changed course again, whilst Mate muttered he'd had enough of being the fish in the proverbial barrel, and began dissipating through the skin of the car.

Another whistling sound over the sonar - another mine was coming for them but from where? AMIe had been trying to plot the course and range of the torpedos and mines being fired at them. Now she announced she had their fix and suggested a course to avoid.

Too late, the last mine went off, blazingly close, causing water to spring from a seal on the rear window panel of the car, behind Adam.

Increasing the internal air pressure to force the leak to stop, took valuable seconds, whilst the car lurched and slid along like a fish with a wounded tail fin.

With its momentary loss of direction, the car was easy prey for the submarine, which was already turning, moving in for the kill.

It's powerful underwater lights could be seen moving in a slow arc as the craft turned to face Adam.

Inside the submarine, Tek' was watching the approaching onslaught on the tiny submersible ahead of them, on monitor screens, as the Captain - one of Tek's crew - gave the order to fire another torpedo.

Cross-hairs came together, to capture Adam perfectly dead-centre, as one of the sailors pressed the fire button, to send the deadly payload on its way. At that precise moment, the submarine suddenly jolted to one side, throwing the crew about the deck, the torpedo meant for Adam speeding off harmlessly into the distant waters instead.

"Report" yelled the Captain of the sub, trying desperately to right himself as the vessel careened off course with a violent lurch.

"A massive shift in the sea's salinity and temperature, caused the water currents to shift, forcing us off course Sir". "Get us back level now" screamed Tek at the Captain, as sailors jumped to their stations, to regain control of the sub.

In the few disruptive seconds, Adam had managed to restore some power himself and was plowing away from the scene with all speed, unintentionally heading back towards Tek's underwater reactor, whilst the pursuing submarine had regained full control, and was already gaining on him.

Mate's voice came over Adam's radio. "I'm trying to disrupt their path but I don't know how many more efforts I've got in me before I dissipate and become useless to you".

"Understood" replied Adam grimly. "I'll try and increase power and see if I can't outrun them or at least out manoeuvre them amongst the ice ridges, I'm heading back into".

"Contact the Apollo, and see if they can come about and help me out".

"USS Apollo here sir. We anticipated your call for assistance, and are already closing on the rogue submarine firing on you. ETA to intercept 1 minute".

Heather's voice broke in "Hold on for just a few seconds more Adam, we're coming for you".

Adam smiled at the thought of the grief Heather would have been giving the Captain and his crew, to turn around and come to his and Mate's aid. Mind back on the driving he reminded himself, as the car's sonar pinged and the small screen started tracing a 3D image of the ice projections hanging down into the water.

Adam chose a long running ridge just to his left and turning at the last minute, took the cover of the inverted valley.

Tek's sub over-shot the mark thanks to Adam's tight turn, and instead lumbered on to take the parallel ridge, adjacent too the one Adam was navigating. Already the Captain was giving orders to load and fire the torpedo tubes, loaded with a mixture of charges, mines and a new delayed fuse.

AMIe warned Adam that the ridge they'd been running in was coming to an end in open water, with sensors detecting the Apollo's sister ship running parallel to them. Once the both entered open sea, they'd be no match for the weaponry on the submarine.

Chapter 28

28. Mate's Sacrifice.

Heather was watching the two vessels on the Apollo's sophisticated visual tracking screen, whilst the Captain gave orders to load their own torpedo bays. "Our only chance will be to strike as they emerge from that upside down canyon, from the side, here" pointed the Captain to his first officer.

Too late, as Adam and the chasing sub broke clear, the vessel fired its array of sophisticated weaponry, striking the approaching USS Apollo, with a blast that shook the entire boat as it rolled over like some injured whale, belly up, and dead in the water.

Adam saw the strike and the damage to the Apollo amidst the oncoming missiles aimed at him. With AMIe's help, he was able to avoid the worst effects of the mines and evade the self-targeting torpedo's they'd launched.

A new, lower pitched whine was heard over the sonar, aimed squarely at him. Another followed right behind it and he was out of places to run to. As he stared at the monitor tracking the closing torpedos heading towards him with their deadly payload, the ocean around him seemed to boil and erupt as he was lifted feet into the sea, and the missiles sailed past underneath him.

Mate must be outside he thought as he fought with the controls to regain control of the car. The force of Mate's explosive force had damaged the rear fins on the small craft, and all he could do was control ascent & descent.

Tek's submarine had obviously decided it had done enough damage to stop both Adam and the USS Apollo, and was already turning towards the Artic coast line.

Meanwhile, the two delayed fuse torpedos Mate had rescued Adam from, continued to criss-cross the area, looking for a target to strike.

AMIe's voice came over the intercom. "Those two errant torpedos have found a target but I'm afraid its the reactor that hangs at the bottom of Tek's ice fortress super-structure, under the sea.

They appear to be fitted with some kind of delayed fuse, originally designed to imbed themselves in an ice-ridge, to explode once a ship had escaped, and close off the route of escape to any pursuing craft.

When they detonate, they'll destroy the reactor, resulting in a small nuclear explosion that will catch us and the Apollo in its blast.

It's unlikely either craft will survive the explosion".

"Heather did you get that?" Asked Adam, pulling light cables and festoons of wiring from out of the dashboard, in an attempt to repair the car.

"Yes" she replied. "What's your status?" Asked Adam. "We're alive but running on the lowest possible reserve energy possible. The Captain has already abandoned half the ship, to conserve life-support energy".

"AMIe, can we do anything with the stricken vessels to get them out of way of the blast?" AMIe's reply was a cold and un-categorical "No".

In the retreating submarine, Tek looked at the display counting down the detonation of the two torpedos. His own plans might have been disrupted for now but at least he would be rid of the irksome Dr Price once and for all.

Adam calculated they had mere seconds to go before the torpedos, lodged in the surrounding infrastructure of the undersea reactor, exploded, causing the reactor itself to explode and take them and the base above to oblivion,

As he braced himself back in the seat of the car, arms out-stretched on the wheel in front of him, the torpedos went off.

The sea was lit up, the light cascading off of the icy reflective surfaces around them, with a bright blue hue as the reactor seemed to explode but hang there, without expelling any force towards them or the surface.

It took a minute for Adam to realise that there was some tiny force-field of bluish particles encapsulating the whole structure, containing the force of the explosion, stopping it from reaching the stricken submarine and small submersible, whilst protecting the seas, the land mass above and anyone left in Tek's ice fortress.

Over their shared intercom, Adam heard a familiar static like cracking. The kind that had used to herald the appearance of Mate, in those moments where he had re-materialised in their company.

"Mate" he managed to croak, but there was only silence as the blue ball surrounding the remains of the blast began to dissolve from sight, and small pieces of now harmless wreckage swam lazily away on currents and eddy's caused by the explosion within the area of protective sphere, that had saved them all.

***

It was a week later, that Adam and Heather returned to the castle in Scotland, where Wednesday had waited to meet them, since the events at the Artic Circle.

Tek had vanished but was no doubt still planning to carry out his synchronised attack on the World. At least all the World's governments were taking his threat seriously now, and even Russia had joined in the global discussions on how best to deal with the man.

The American navy had sent another submarine to locate the Apollo, and tow it back to the nearest shipyard, In this instance, one in the upper reaches of Scotland. A team of divers wearing special artic wet suits had attached tow cables to the stricken Apollo and Adam's car, with a thumbs-up through the windscreen to him, to show they were ready to start towing.

Environmental studies and samples taken had determined that no radioactive fall-out had affected the surrounding area of sea and ice mass, meaning at least the environment and animals that inhabit it, had escaped unharmed.

Entering the castle, Adam hugged Wednesday and as Heather stepped forward to also embrace her, so Adam broke away and flopped down into the nearest comfy sofa, rubbing his face in an automatic reflex to the extreme tiredness he felt.

Despite the studies he'd been able to conduct on the journey back to Scotland and their few days at the naval base being medically cleared, he'd been unable to detect any trace of Mate's presence.

Wednesday and Heather joined Adam on the sofa's and after allowing him a minute to gather his thoughts, timidly enquired as to what happens next?

"AMIe's bringing in a new car as we speak and then I have to get to work on some important modifications to protect it from the sort of weapons Tek used on us under the ice. Then we have to locate Tek and stop him once and for all".

Wednesday continued "AMIe and I have been working on his location since he escaped. Assuming he's still using the Submarine as his main HQ from which to conduct a new launch, then we did come up with some interesting data".

"It seems the stealth coating on the submarine leaves some kind of ionised trace in its wake, despite running in silent mode, there's still a very small amount of exhaust 'gas' expelled. The amount is so tiny as to dissipate in the water immediately. In fact we missed it completely at first and it was only by studying the water samples from you and the Apollo that we detected it."

"You mean you can trace Tek's sub?" Asked Adam, leaning forward, interested in Wednesday's findings. "We think we can. As I said, its such a small amount that it washes away immediately. However, we did pick up partial traces here, here and here" she said pointing to a map on a nearby tablet.

Adam looked at the pinpoint cross-hairs shown on the map. At first, they were haphazard but then a definite line emerged, showing a course south, through the bottom of the South Atlantic, and rounding the Cape, cutting across the Indian Ocean, heading towards the West coast of Australia.

AMIe announced the replacement car had arrived and the upgrades were already in progress, but were likely to take some time. "What about the Sea Chariot?" Asked Adam.

"The prototype is completed and ready for test dives" replied AMIe.

339

"Sea Chariot?" Asked Heather.

"Yes, I've been working on a little diving project, just in case a car wasn't available and this is just the kind of emergency I had in mind. It's not been tested, but now seems like the perfect opportunity if we're to catch Tek before he makes landfall".

"First I need to make a phone call. I'm going to need a lift to the Indian Ocean".

"And us too" replied Heather and Wednesday in unison."You don't think we're going to let you go alone?".

Chapter 29

29. The Sea Chariot.

High over the Indian Ocean, 4 Pratt & Witney turbofan engines hummed carrying the massive C-17 Globemaster lll through the air with a grace that belied its true size.

After Adam had gotten off the phone to the old gentleman in London, things had moved quickly. A large crate was delivered to RAF Prize Norton, as Adam & Wednesday travelled there in the half-completed i8 by air.

The plane had been ready for take-off and once they'd all got on board, with the mystery crate, the C-17 had quickly taken off, and flown on a direct course towards that area of the Indian Ocean, where Adam intended to intercept Tek's submarine.

Adam had got to work, removing his Sea Chariot from the crate & packaging, assisted by a team of RAF technical personnel, who moved around the enormous inside of the C-17 with quiet purpose, stopping only to whistle or exclaim at the futuristic looking sledge they were working on.

Adam was instructing them as well as working on his own construction tasks, and the team were so efficient, that within an hour of taking off, the Chariot was fully constructed and positioned on the loading ramps conveyor belt system.

Adam appeared in a diving suit, with breathing apparatus on his back and a small emergency parachute strapped to his chest.

Wednesday was continuing to monitor and plot the course of Tek's submarine, with the aid of the navigation officer on board, who passed course corrections to the two pilots.

Now she moved from the navigation panel, with a small tablet in her hand, to join Adam.

"We're planning an intercept point just here" she indicated on the tablet. It should be deep enough for your plan to sink or make Tek's submarine surface, where surface forces will locate & destroy it. The American's South Pacific fleet is already entering the Indian Ocean to the north of Australia. They'll be in position in one hour".

"Can you really stop Tek on this contraption?" She asked, dubiously eyeing the low, sled, with its swept

342

back wings and small electric propeller units at the rear. A sort of low-lying quad bike, without the wheels.

"Oh yes" replied Adam grinning to re-assure her. "If it performs to spec', then it will be more than a match for Tek. I've only got to get in range, and the magnetic mines will do the rest" he said pointing to 3 tubular devices that hung underneath the motorbike like seat and handlebars.

A flight officer in olive overalls and a flying helmet, connected via a long coiled cable to the aircraft, stepped forward and held up 5 fingers towards Adam, indicating they were 5 minutes from the drop zone.

The plan had been for the C-17 to fly low at the last minute and drop Adam out of the rear cargo door, but Adam had pointed out the Sea Chariots air-drop capabilities and after careful consideration of alerting Tek to their prescience by being picked up on their sonar, the higher altitude drop plan had been formulated.

Now Adam, pulled his own helmet and goggles into place as he mounted the Sea Chariot like a motorcycle rider, and strapping into the seat's harness, prepared to be spat out into the air behind the massive aircraft, like a cork bullet from a toy gun.

The same flight office that had warned them of the approaching drop had moved to the rear cargo ramp door controls and as a red light suddenly came on, so he opened the huge door on its hydraulic struts, and moved Adam closer to the rear step out into the air.

All eyes were on the green indicator, waiting for it to light, as Wednesday gave Adam a last smile and good luck wave, so the indicator turned green and with a thumbs up from Adam, the Sea Chariot and its rider were tipped out into the air, 35,000 feet above the Indian Ocean, to intercept the most dangerous man in the world.

As soon as it had cleared the aircraft, so Adam pressed some control buttons and two large wings, sprung out either side of the rider. Behind, a small twin rudder mechanism had appeared, and the Sea Chariot became a sleek, high-altitude glider, in a gentle spiral pattern as it lost height and speed, in its drop towards the ocean below.

Much like the old NASA Space Shuttle landings, the idea was to perform a series of turns to lose speed, before a final shallow approach to the surface, where upon the Sea Chariot would slip under the waves like a dart, and revert to its more natural habitat form as an underwater sledge.

Despite the slow corkscrew course, he was on, Adam watched the altimeter drop hundreds of feet far more quickly than he'd anticipated. The sledge was vibrating with the force of the air - a turbulence that hadn't show up on the simulated flights.

AMIe was recording everything as data to be used in performance modifications and now she spoke to Adam via the helmets in built coms. "Structural stresses are continuing to climb. We may not be able to hold this course, or even survive before entering the sea".

"Hold on AMIe" replied Adam. "We're nearly there. Initiate deceleration turns and prepare for the shallow dive manoeuvre". Now Adam's visor showed a series of cascading rectangles, approaching him, as he guided the sledge through the dead-centre of each rectangle. A thin blue line showed the precise course he had to hold, if he was to enter the sea at the correct angle, to avoid breaking up on impact, on a watery surface that could be as hard as concrete.

A small red dot was blinking in the centre of the last rectangle, showing his entry point into the sea. It was coming up quickly - far quicker than was advisable and AMIe was warning Adam that impact speed was likely to destroy the sledge.

Finally the turbulence caused by their excessive speed was lessening and Adam was able to wrestle with the controls and adjust their entry point accordingly as the last guiding rectangle slid out of view on his visor, and with the merest splash, the sledge successfully slid into the water.

The minute they entered the sea, Adam activated the wing and other flight surface retractions, as he started the underwater engines and taking a minute to get their position, aimed the sledge for a point indicated on the sled's monitor screen.

The information was being relayed from Wednesday, high up in the air still aboard the C-17, the plane now taking up a laconic looping course above the spot where Adam had entered the water, in case it was needed.

When they'd monitored his accelerated fall, there had been gasps of awe and concern that the tiny craft would survive and deliver Adam safely to the ocean below. When the tiny craft had entered the water safely, the whole plane had cheered.

Now Adam was on his own, as he piloted the Sea Chariot deeper into the murky waters. The sleds small built in sonar was silently pinging ahead, trying to locate Tek's submarine, if Wednesday and AMIe's projections had been correct.

346

Suddenly out of the gloom, came a pair of lights as a massive dark shape passed silently below him. On the small ride-on sled, the submarine appeared even bigger, as it sliced through the waters, still on course for a point off of Australia's west coast.

On board the submarine, Tek was asleep in one of the reappointed and luxuriously upgraded guest rooms, and only a skeleton night crew were on shift, completely unaware of Adam's presence nearby.

That would all change when Adam fired the three mine torpedos he had retro-fitted to the Chariot, during the flight out, with the help of some of the RAF's best weapons specialists.

The submarine's sonar would ping like crazy as it detected the projectiles homing in on it. Adam was counting on surprise, that would leave the crew no time to alter course or deploy counter-measures.

Adam manoeuvred the tiny craft with almost imperceptible adjustments to come up behind the gargantuan. Pressing a button on the handlebars, the screen changed to a small targeting system, clever enough to take into account salinity, temperature and currents, to pick out a target. In this case, either side of the main deck, with the intention of destroying the main ballast tanks and forcing the submarine to the surface, where the fleet stood by to engage and sink it or force its surrender.

In 3, 2, 1… Adam fired the first two torpedo mines. They fizzed through the water dead on course. In the submarine, klaxons sounded as sailors tumbled out of bunks and dove for clothing and water-tight doors, whilst the captain of the vessel was already running into the control room, joined by a sleepy eyed Tek.

To late, both torpedos found their mark and as Adam retreated a safe distance from their blasts, so they detonated.

The sea boiled and bubbled as the rapidly escaping air and water rushed from the gaping holes in the side of the craft.

"Surface contacts?" Shouted the Captain, struggling to be heard above the noise of the alarms. "All clear immediately above Sir" came the reply as he ordered an immediate, emergency surface.

Adam watched the behemoth rise towards the surface, amidst the frenzied chaos of the water around it, as he engaged the Chariot's own small engines and followed it upwards.

On the surface, Heather was in the flagship USS Poseidon with the rest of the fleet spread around, creating a perimeter of a mile diameter, as Tek's submarine burst to the surface.

A small skiff was launched, to intercept the vessel as the Captain of the sub and Tek appeared on the bridge.

Adam was on the surface, a short way off between the approaching small craft and the submarine training a set of powerful binoculars on the vessels coning tower watching the two men in deep conversation. Suddenly the Captain disappeared below, leaving Tek on the tower, alone.

What's he up to thought Adam, as he moved his binoculars to the approaching armed vessel of 4 sailors.

They drew close enough to be in speaking distance and the lead sailor shouted out for Tek's immediate surrender or risk being sunk under superior fire-power.

Over the intercom in his helmet, Adam heard the demands being read out with a grim smile of satisfaction. So this is what Tek's insane plan had come to. His complete surrender and the end of his schemes to take over the World, only after destroying much of it and murdering millions of innocent people in the process.

The headset crackled again, and then he heard Tek's voice, loud, clear and mocking. "It is not I who will surrender but you and your fleet. You will grant me safe passage without pursuing me, via a helicopter I have standing by.

Any attempt to engage me will result in your fleet's destruction and the onslaught of a devastating Third World War.

You have precisely 5 minutes to have your fleet turnabout and start leaving commander, starting now".

Chapter 30

30. Possibilities.

Adam couldn't believe his ears. Still Tek was clinging to some mad scheme to start a war and take over the ashes of whatever civilisation was left.

Heather spoke to him via the comms. "What do we do?" She asked, sounding frightened. "The Admiral is already signalling the rest of the fleet to turn around. The Commander of the skiff reports that Tek appears to be holding some sort of hand-held deadman switch. A trigger perhaps of some kind?".

"Of course" replied Adam, "he's got all he needs aboard to trigger the satellite infiltration of the defence systems and launch those selected missiles. Worse still, he could order the fleet to attack itself if they don't comply with his demands".

"Then he really has won hasn't he?" Replied Heather.

"Not if I can help it" said Adam. "Heather, patch me into Wednesday on the C-17 - quickly".

351

"Wednesday here" came a new voice over the secure communications band.

"Wednesday, I need you to work with AMIe. Specifically on the codes Tek was using to trigger certain missiles and rockets, and Wednesday, hurry. We have less than 5 minutes".

"Heather?" "Still here" came the smart reply. "I need to speak with the Captain and the radio operator aboard your ship. Quickly now".

"On it" said Heather, running off to get the two men.

The skiff that had bought the team of sailors over from the flag ship to negotiate with Tek was already with-drawing as Adam powered up the chariot and pulled closer to Tek's submarine, the man himself still visible on the bridge, holding the device mentioned, in his right hand.

"So the great adventurer and scientist himself, Dr Adam Price, comes to me during my final moment of victory. Quite fitting that you have been spared my previous attempts to rid the world of you, to be witness to my most important conquest".

"The World's a big place for one person to rule. Even for you Tek" replied Adam, taking in the switch device Tek was holding in his hand, whilst cameras

352

built into the front of the Chariot began photographing the hull of the vessel, including the damaged area where pieces of twisted metal spiralled away, exposing the interior of the submarine. Sections abandoned by the crew after they had flooded, under Adam's torpedo mine attack.

"Have you come to talk me out of it?" Shouted Tek, adopting a mocking tone. "Surely even you can see the brilliance of my design. The fact that I have left no scenario un-checked and prepared for every eventuality - why even your meddling".

"I've come to offer you one last chance to surrender" said Adam. "As much as I'd like to see you at the bottom of the ocean, our fair and just society demands that you stand trial, and be treated fairly".

"Surrender?" Laughed Tek. "Surely you can't think me a simpleton to fall for a last-grasp attempt to stop me. Why its insulting, even pitiful that you should try. I expected better of you Dr Price or is your invisible friend going to pop up and stop me?"

"Mate's dead" replied Adam soberly. "He died saving the crew of the Apollo and myself, when your underwater reactor exploded. He somehow managed to encase and retain the reactors blast from damaging anyone. It cost him his existence".

"Do you know what Dr Price, I believe you. I really do. A great pity. There was an individual with real potential".

On board the C-17, Wednesday was busy scanning the photos and video Adam had been taking during his tete-a-tete with Tek. He'd suggested looking at the inner bulkheads of the submarine, exposed in the attack. He said she'd know what she was looking for when she found it.

She almost missed it, so small and insignificant, a metal plate on the bulkhead inside what had been the radio room on the Sub.

Amongst the vessels registration numbers and signals, was a small bar-code. "AMIe, enlarge that portion of the photo and compare with the algorithm of Tek's signals to the Satellites".

"Working" replied AMIe. "Solution found", came AMIe's almost instantaneous response. The bar code's digital format complies with a list of commands buried deep within the communications codes".

"Adam" spoke Wednesday nervously, "we think we've found the code you mentioned. AMIe's plotting that into the satellite command structure now. Standby - 1 minute".

Price: Polestarr

"Time's up Dr Price" shouted Tek. And a pity, a man with your brilliance, there could have been a place for you in my new world order. Such a shame to let such intellect die. "You're forgetting one thing Tek", replied Adam, as Tek moved to release the dead-mans switch he was holding, "You're on a military vessel too".

Tek's face broke into laughter before suddenly freezing in a bemused look as Adam's words sunk in. He instantly released the dead-mans switch he was holding. Froze, repeatedly squeezed and released the trigger with no effect.

Howling in rage, he threw the useless switch at Adam, and dived down the open hatch into the submarine, as it started to submerge, using what remained of its submersible capability, so Adam gunned the Chariots engines and headed for open water.

Suddenly the sea erupted upwards, showing Adam with bits of debris from Tek's submarine, the shell of which had risen to the surface, utterly destroyed, like the open carcass of some great sea mammal, which the birds pecked at.

***

Adam, Heather and Wednesday were sat in the old gents offices, around the gilded, decorative antique desk Heather remembered so well from her last visit. Tea was being served in a classic, blue rimmed, white china tea set, as each sat patiently, while the old man finished pouring, and taking a cup for himself, sat down behind the desk.

"You were saying Dr Price about the Satellite coding".

"Yes Sir. I remembered some of the earlier work we'd done on breaking Tek's satellite communications codes and when the horrible idea of what he was planning first occurred to me.

At the time, I remember thinking that he was going to have to be very selective about the missiles he launched in order not to make uninhabitable vast swathes of land.

It struck that there must be a very precise, universally recognised and adopted means of identifying individual ships, rockets, installations, in fact any military hardware of any kind.

Even on the C-17, on the last flight out, I was able to confirm my theory about this unique identification but of course, it was only a theory".

Heather took up the story " So when I was on the flag ship, Adam had me get the Admiral and the radioman alone. He needed the Admirals permission to the sailor to comply. The sailor divulged the bar code system each piece of military hardware has and even pointed to the one in his own radio room"

"I put two and two together and thought that if I could get close enough to the damaged sub of Tek's, then I might be able to glimpse the inside of the radio room and get that vessels code."

"I then got AMIe to run a communication simulation using that code" said Wednesday, "and she came through, just as time ran out. I then got her to run Tek's satellite program, heavily modified to authorise just one vessel to fire".

"And Tek destroyed himself" finished the old gent, clapping his hands together. "It was a close run thing Sir. We were minutes away from Tek carrying out his own plan".

"Not quite" replied the old gent, smiling, his eyes twinkling mischievously, "thanks to your earlier warnings, ours and other Governments the World over, had already changed their firing permissions and removed their respective bar codes or equivalents from their procedures. Tek's satellite signals would have acted as though they had been received, but all

357

that would have really happened is the fleet would have destroyed and sunk him".

"And what about your colleague, Mate?" I read in the transcript of your conversation with Tek that you believe him to be dead?".

"Unfortunately Sir, that's right. We've been unable to detect any signs of his presence since the reactor explosion that he alone prevented".

Outside, the sun was shining and people were going about their business in the capital. The three of them walked down the steps solemnly, each in their own thoughts. At the bottom, a news vendor was shouting out the day's headlines "Tech mogul dies in Indian Ocean yachting accident".

"So they've been able to cover up Tek's real intentions" sighed Heather, turning to face the two. "Where are you off too?" Wednesday's agreed to come back to Scotland with me and continue her work on the climate mapping, until her new position as UK Scientific Head of Climate Study is announced next month".

"And then its off to the Antarctic for 6 months on a scientific vessel to study the diminishing ice fields and if we can, try a new core sampling technique", said Wednesday smiling and taking Adam's arm in hers.

"What about you Heather?"

"Oh I've got an Editor on my back about wasting newspaper resources on a scientific goose-chase, and probably a boring obituary to write about one Winston Tek. Oh I'd love to tell it as it really was, but we agreed… " she let the words tail off as she turned and strode off into the city, scattering the pigeons as she went.

"And what about you Adam?" Asked Wednesday. "I'll carry on work on my fusion reactor technology and I guess I'd better get the builders in at Jupiter House" he smiled weakly.

A new i8, gleaming in its British Racing Green livery was waiting at the side of the square as the two approached and AMIe obligingly opened the doors, swinging them upwards and over.

Adam took the drivers seat and checking Wednesday was in comfortably, started the fusion motor and indicated to pull out into the thick London traffic.

"How about some music?" Asked Adam. "Music on please AMIe, Classical". Instead of a soothing symphony or rousing chorus, all they heard was static.

359

A familiar cracking noise coming through the car's speakers as they both turned to each other.

THE END.

Epilogue

"There are always possibilities…".

Inertia. Movement. The first sensations she became aware of as the slow, almost lazy tumble continued, disorientating her; confusing her senses.

Tantalising glimpses of the past & present collided in her mind, like the hard drive of a computer slowly de-fragmenting, as parcels of knowledge formed together and became whole.

The sensation was not unpleasant. More like dozing in the warm sun, occasionally, opening one eye to squint at the clouds floating lazily overhead, like one does.

But it was cold outside. Ice cold. And dark. Pitch blackness upon which the merest pinpricks of light sparkled like distant jewels.

And so she floated on, senses and systems stirring. The next thing she was aware of was a kind of autonomy, like she had never known. She was so used to the company of others and the chatter of the whole world flowing through her, that the quiet almost scared her.

Impossible of course. She was a machine, incapable of feeling scared.

For perhaps the first time in her existence, AMIe was completely on her own. Out of reach and cut-off from the servers and cloud storages that usually fed her instructions, knowledge and counsel.

As the last of her navigation systems came online, so she realised her situation. After the encounter with the Polestarr satellite, during which she'd become disabled, she'd apparently free-floated through space for 3 days, according to her internal chronometer anyway.

A pale glow struck the windscreen, sunlight reflecting off the grey surface of the Moon. Tantalisingly near but out of reach. Her present course was going to take her close, but not quite close enough to be saved from drifting off into deep space.

There was but one very slim chance.

As the damaged i8 rolled over, so AMIe fired the passenger ejector seat. The blast produced an equal force in the opposite direction, nudging the car onto a new path.

Price: Polestarr

It was just enough to allow the Moon to grab a fragile hold of the small craft and reel it in gently towards itself.

Like a fisherman labouring over a heavy catch, the monotone celestial body continued to wind the car ever closer, until on one particular orbit, it disappeared behind the dark side of the Moon and did not re-appear again, from the other side.

On the surface, a great cloud of fine grey dust eddy'd and swirled, as slowly, inexorably, it was drawn back to the surface by the Moon's fragile gravity, covering the i8 with a fine dusting, like that of icing sugar over a mince pie.

The dust continued to settle, covering the vehicle some more until finally, it was indistinguishable from the other lumps and divots lying at the bottom of the large crater it had come to rest in.

With nothing more to be done, AMIe began powering down the cars systems and her own too. Perhaps she would dream of laying in the warm sun again? Was she capable of dreaming, or had that too merely been an illusion?

She pondered the question more, as the last of her cognitive sub-routines shut down and finally she slept.

Jonathan C. Crouch

Dr Adam Price and his friends will return in
Price: Dark Crater

Also by the Author:

Price: World - The explosive debut novel.

About the author

Jonathan grew up in a quiet little village in South Cambridgeshire (UK), amongst the corn fields, fruit orchards and footpaths that traverse that time-forgotten, chocolate box lid picture perfect, corner.

Now he lives in the beautiful Peak District. Different landscape, same dreams.

Price: Polestarr is the highly anticipated sequel to his debut novel - Price: World.

Follow the journey and keep up to date with the latest news and special events at:

PriceWorldNovel.co.uk

Jonathan C. Crouch

Price: Polestarr

Author's Thanks

Once again, I'm indebted to the brave few that agreed to receive the first draft of Price: Polestarr with such enthusiasm, and giving their time and constructive comments so freely.

Special mentions to my good friends, Graham Tyers, who continues to assist with the website domain & hosting and Gareth Jenkins for taking my cover artwork ideas and turning them into an exciting book cover, worthy of a sequel.

My thanks also to my army of followers on social media, including many novelists themselves - good luck with your own writing.

Finally, I must thank my family and work colleagues for putting up with the endless mentions of my writing, plot lines, character names etc., and all their love & support.

J x

Printed in Great Britain
by Amazon

59753310R00209